*Not Flowers,*
*but Love*

# Not Flowers, but Love

KRYS BATTS

ISBN: 0996321101
ISBN 13: 9780996321105
Cover design by Robin Ludwig Design Inc.
http://www.gobookcoverdesign.com/

*This novel is dedicated to my grandmothers, two brilliant,*
*loving women who I know are watching over me.*
*I hope that they're both smiling proudly as well.*

*Truth*

*Set your words to the truth,*
*A tune not always sweet to hear,*
*And yet the most enduring rhapsody ever*
*To be written, to be spoken, irrevocably sincere.*

*Allow your tongue to connect with your heart,*
*For there lies your honest humanity.*
*And though vulnerability may render you shaken,*
*Your yearning spirit will finally be free.*

*If words may be music,*
*Then your voice is the instrument,*
*Your soul the composer, your mind the audience.*
*Listen to the song that sings within you,*
*That eternal truth that wants you to dance!*

*I've heard it said that love is*
*a many-splintered thing...*

# CHAPTER 1

*O beautiful sunlight!*
*Without thee, all the brilliant blooms would perish.*

IT WAS THE last day of their weekend getaway in San Francisco, but a heavy storm had rumbled in and delayed their flights home—his to Miami and hers to Houston. As the morning was still young and the daylight shadowed by smoke-colored clouds, they had decided to stay in bed, their naked bodies intertwined, his face lying gently atop hers as they listened to the soft tap of rain against their august hotel-room window.

Jamie liked it here in this place, snuggled up against Ken's solid six-foot frame. If she wasn't careful, she could get used to this—the pleasant feeling of comfort and belonging with this man. She could lose herself in the sensations he evoked simply by holding her and placing his large palms securely around her back and waist. And she especially enjoyed these moments of serene quiet when it was almost as if the rest of the world ceased to exist. All that remained was this dim room that they shared, tucked so nicely away, with their limbs carelessly entangled. Neither of them was complaining that the storm had prevented their immediate return to their busy lives. There would be plenty of time for the hustle and bustle that awaited them.

"I don't want to go back." Ken broke the silence and pulled her more tightly against him. Her back was pressed skin to skin against his chest, and she smiled a satisfied smile that he couldn't see. "I just want to stay right here in this bed with you. It's like being on a remote island somewhere."

"I was just thinking the same thing." Jamie rolled over to face him and pressed her nose lightly against his before kissing it. "But our real lives are waiting for us."

"Yeah, I know." He sighed and turned onto his back.

"What's wrong?" She placed a hand on his chest and ran her fingers downward before rubbing his abdomen. He was built like a rock. There was absolutely no fat to be found on his exquisite body.

"Nothing's wrong. I've just got a lot going on, a lot of changes to manage."

"Stuff at work?"

"Yeah, it's always work."

She leaned down to slowly brush her lips against his. She then kissed his ear before whispering, "Don't think about any of that right now. Think about me."

Ken chuckled, rolled back over, and encased her in his arms once more. He then kissed her forehead before delivering his own special attention to each of her lips individually. "Just remember—you asked for it."

Jamie laughed delightedly as his mouth covered hers. Then his body covered hers. And the rain that she knew was still tapping against the window suddenly seemed like a world away because she was aware of only the feeling of Ken's body merging with her own.

She could get used to this. She definitely could. But she wouldn't. She would never say to herself that her relationship with Ken was anything more than casual and convenient for them both. When they had met at an energy-industry conference several months earlier, she had been immediately drawn to him—his polished carriage, his keen intellect, and, of course, his chiseled build. But she wasn't in the market for a serious relationship then or now, having already endured a series of calamities otherwise known as her love life. Now she had sworn off fantasies of marriage and the whole white-picket-fence thing...at least for the time being.

Jamie moaned with pleasure as Ken adeptly plunged so deep inside her that she swore she could feel him in her stomach. She would allow herself to thoroughly enjoy this moment of sweet surrender to his commanding prowess. She gave herself permission to do that. But tomorrow, when she was back at work and restored to a universe that was completely separate from his, she would stuff down this reckless abandon and all of the perils that could come with it. Tomorrow, Ken would once again be a toy that she had taken out of the box to play with for a short while before returning it safely to that box, stored away in a dark corner of herself along with all the past heartbreaks that she had tried so hard to bury.

Three weeks later, Jamie was reposed in her office, the time with Ken in San Francisco now efficiently deposited to her memory bank. Her return to the office grind accompanied her sense of being restored to the way of life that she had come to thrive on. Anyone who knew her well knew Jamie was a relentless workaholic with a penchant for mining details and delivering precise facts. A lesser-known aspect was her abiding antipathy to flowers. Her bias was in no way frivolous or accidental but rather correlative to her dating history. At age thirty-five, she was certain that she had dated every no-good man to be found, and most of them had come bearing some sort of flower, a supposed affirmation of their goodwill and devotion. But the illusion of some special romantic bond had always quickly faded, giving way to her paramours' less-than-honorable intentions, which at times left her twisting in the wind. After an array of such disappointments, she had finally figured out that men's affections were equally as fleeting as the life of the flowers they so casually gifted—and so the flowers truly meant nothing. They held no promise of faithfulness and love. They could not be relied upon as symbols of the bearers' uncommon sense of dedication. She knew that now. And she would be fooled no more by the deceptive blooms, whatever type or shade they came in. She would no longer chase the supposedly ideal blueprint for timeless love and a fulfilled life. Instead, Jamie had decided to channel her energy into her work—into tasks and outcomes that she could control. And—unlike her love life—this bet had paid off, eventually landing her a vice-president role at Radian Energy, a prominent electric company located in downtown Houston, where she had now worked for several years. Her job was not glamorous, but it was certainly critical, as her team was responsible for ensuring that expenses and revenues played well together, among other things. And she was good at it. She had mastered a balancing act that had rattled most of her predecessors, a fact that gave her immense satisfaction.

Now alone in her office, Jamie folded one slender, black-stocking-clad leg over the other and peered at the sun as it barely hung onto its precarious perch in the sky. The fiery-orange orb was fading into dark shades of red as it slowly descended to the edges of the earth. Observing from her expansive office window, Jamie appreciated the size and beauty of the life-sustaining solar neighbor, without which there could be no survival, no humanity, no Jamie. Reminding herself of this fact served to also remind her of her own smallness in comparison to everything else in the vast possible universe. And if she could be so tiny, so miniscule as to be practically invisible, then so too could be her problems.

She shifted in her chair before slowly running the palm of her hand across the back of her dark, short hair. Before long, the motion brought her hand back to its original position on the plush leather armrest. She then cast a forlorn gaze downward from her eighth-floor view to the pretzel of freeways conveniently located a stone's throw from her office building. Unsurprisingly, there was hardly any traffic now, as tomorrow was Thanksgiving, and most people were at airports, either preparing to depart or collecting friends and family who were arriving during one of the most heavily traveled holidays of the year. As she did each year, Jamie would spend the occasion with her own family in Houston, the thought of which momentarily triggered her joy for the season despite her gloomy mood.

"Jamie, you're a machine! Sometimes I think you must have a cot hidden somewhere in here so you can sleep at the office."

She bristled when she heard the voice. It was Jacob Bradley, the VP of sales and marketing and a peer she had once regarded as a trustworthy friend. But unbeknownst to him, word had recently reached Jamie that Jacob had become a problem for her. According to Katrina Murphy, the training department manager who doubled as a scandalmonger, Jacob had mentioned a concern to their boss that Jamie was in over her head. Unfortunately, Katrina didn't know the reason for his allegation, so Jamie wasn't yet sure of what to do with the grapevine information. Nevertheless, she was deeply stung by his backstabbing and could think of very few people she less preferred to speak with at this particular moment. But she was stuck. Pasting on her best Mona Lisa smile, she wheeled her chair around to face Jacob.

"Sometimes it feels like I do live here. Are you heading home now?" He had his briefcase in hand, so she already knew the answer.

"Yep. Just wanted to wish you a great holiday before I left. You're going to your mom's house as usual, right?"

"You know it. I hope that you also enjoy the holiday with your family." *Now get out*, she thought to herself.

"Thanks." He remained perfectly still as they silently regarded each other. The moment soon became awkward before he finally spoke again. "Jamie, before I go, I've been meaning to ask you something. Do you mind?"

"No, go right ahead." She confidently leaned back into her chair.

"You know that we've launched a few new products in the past several months. And most of them are performing as expected. But the Postern product isn't doing too well despite our customer volumes hitting the projected targets. Has your team figured out what's going on with that?"

"Ivan is looking into it. We're all seeing the same trends on the same reports, but the root cause is pretty puzzling. We're hoping to get to the bottom of it when Ivan gets back from vacation next week." Ivan, along with half of the company's employees, had taken the entire holiday week off.

"OK, that's good to know. I'm sure that you're all over it." He smiled, seeming relieved.

"Of course. That's my job."

"Awesome." He continued to look at her as though searching for something more to say. Since Jamie wasn't feeling especially charitable, she chose to simply return his look in silence again. For reasons that were a mystery to her, this man had decided to take her down and had been dumb

enough to think that she wouldn't hear about it. Sheer professionalism protected him from her wrath—for now.

Under her blank gaze, Jacob finally spoke again. "I'll
head out, then. Thanks for your help, Jamie." He walked
toward the door just as Michael Collins, a very nice-
looking mailroom clerk, appeared.

"Hi. I hope that I'm not interrupting."

"Hi, Michael. Come on in." Jamie was relieved for a
reason to turn her attention from Jacob, who again extended his holiday wishes before finally leaving.

"Working late again?"

She smiled warmly. "I guess that I should ask you
the same thing." Michael was always so shy with her that
she had months earlier guessed that he nursed a small
crush. But at around age twenty-one, he was much too
young for Jamie. And coworkers, as a general rule, were
off-limits in her mind. She had already been burned several years ago when she had dated a colleague at a different company. She would never make that particular
mistake again.

Michael held up a stack of overnight packages and
returned her smile. "I'm making my last run for express
mail. Holidays don't matter much to the mailroom. We
don't leave until every package is on its way. Do you have
anything that needs to go out tonight?"

"No, I don't. Thank you." Jamie rested her elbows on
her polished oak desk and leaned forward slightly. "Will
you be seeing your family during the holiday?"

"No, ma'am. My family is in Michigan. I'll probably stay in or play a little basketball with some friends. I haven't decided yet."

"Aw, that's too bad." Ordinarily, she would have invited him to have dinner with her family, but she didn't want to risk blurring any lines in their professional rapport.

"To be honest, I'm looking forward to watching the football games, Miss Dubois. I'll see my family at Christmas."

"I see." She nodded, surprised that he didn't mention a girlfriend. "Be safe, and enjoy the long weekend."

He began to back up to exit her office. "Thank you, Miss Dubois. You do the same."

"All right, Michael. Happy Thanksgiving." Jamie couldn't help smirking as she watched him stumble while continuing to walk backward. It was obvious that being around her made him nervous.

"Happy Thanksgiving!" He finally reached the corridor and practically scurried out of view with a wave of his hand.

In the renewed silence, Jamie eventually grew restless with her solitude, so she shut down her computer and packed a thick stack of documents into her satchel. She then used her cell phone to call her mother while walking to the building garage. Part of her annual routine was to inquire as to whether Mama needed any help cooking the turkey or stuffing. Unsurprisingly, Mama had it all under control with the help of Jamie's younger sister, Layla.

The two women loved to cook, whereas Jamie grimaced at merely boiling water, a fact that Mama always considered when Jamie made her halfhearted offer to help with the Thanksgiving feast. So as with most nights, Jamie would spend the evening with her bosom buddy Bear, a rust-colored Pomeranian. She might also make a few calls to extend holiday wishes to some friends. Tomorrow afternoon, she would drive by a grocery store to pick up some sort of dessert, maybe a few pumpkin pies, to take to her mother's house for a festive spread that usually extended across three picnic-size tables since most family members brought their own contributions to the Thanksgiving meal. She was looking forward to the long weekend. It was exactly what she needed to decompress and release all of the steam that the office trials had generated inside her.

When Jamie arrived at her mother's large two-story house the following day, she needed several minutes to find a parking space, as many family members' cars already filled the circular driveway as well as lined the blocks closest to the house. In the end, Jamie was forced to park her white Lexus coupe a couple of blocks away and walk the short distance. She didn't mind, though, since Texas weather tended to be reasonably warm in November. She inhaled deeply, enjoying the gentle breeze that caressed her skin as she headed toward the house with five large pumpkin pies in hand.

Jamie had been raised in this neighborhood, which was once a hot spot for prosperous African-American families. She recalled the meticulous condition of all the homes when she was a child. The yards had all been manicured, the paint fresh. Now as she walked to her mother's house, Jamie noted for the hundredth time that many homes had fallen into disrepair, the owners having allowed the once-pristine coats of paint to chip away, some wooden-board sidings to unceremoniously rot and dangle by a weathered nail or two, and bunches of raggedy weeds to almost over-take the landscaping. But the starkest difference was the empty streets. There was not one child to be seen riding a bicycle or walking a dog. No mothers standing guard over toddlers or preschoolers playing with toys in the front yards. And the silence was absolute. It was as though all the children of Jamie's generation had been the last to in-habit this neighborhood, and when they had grown up and left, they had drained all the life from the veins, leaving behind an ugly corpse. Jamie marveled at how poorly time had treated her childhood terrain, although the pleasant memories remained safely untarnished.

Upon rounding the corner to approach her mother's house, life suddenly sprang from nowhere. At least a dozen adult relatives were gathered in the front yard and drinking from cups of punch or beer while catching up on their lives as others chased giggling children. A handful of Jamie's cousins were sitting on parked cars, watching the activities and trading jokes. The sight of it all lifted her soul, and she happily hugged several family members before entering her mother's home, whereupon she was immediately surrounded by three of her aunts. They clutched and fussed over her as though she was still the three-year-old child that they had taken turns babysitting, and Jamie enjoyed the attention. After several minutes of their clucking, she made her way to the kitchen, where her mother and sister were still cooking.

"Hey, Mama. Where do you want me to put these pies?"

"Put 'em down over there." She pointed to a spot on one of the kitchen counters that was already full of other desserts. "There's no room on any of the tables in the dining room."

Jamie obeyed her mother's instructions and then washed and dried her hands at the kitchen sink while acknowledging her sister. "Layla, you look like you've been up cooking all night!"

"I got a little sleep. Don't worry about me." Layla smiled as she approached Jamie with open arms. "Happy Thanksgiving!"

The sisters had hardly embraced before their mother commanded, "Jamie, get over here and give me a hug." One of Mama's hands continued to stir a pot of gravy while the other was now squeezing her petite hip. Again obedient, Jamie swiftly released her sister and rushed over to her mother with a huge smile.

"Sorry, Mama." They held each other tightly, as though weeks instead of days had passed since they had last seen each other. But time for pleasantries was short, as the designated serving hour was fast approaching. Layla checked on the dinner rolls in the oven and then solicited Jamie's help to distribute the last batch of side dishes to the dining room.

Once back among the hungry crowd, Jamie glanced around the room for Layla's husband, Paul. Failing to spot him, she tapped Layla's shoulder and asked quietly, "Where's Paul?"

A tired expression immediately shadowed Layla's face again as she flapped a hand in the air. "Oh, he's around here somewhere. Probably out by the pool with the kids." She and Paul were parents to two children, an eight-year-old named Sadie and a six-year-old named Luke, both of whom were extremely precocious and spoiled rotten by the family. At the news of Paul's attendance, Jamie involuntarily turned her nose up with disgust. He had never held down steady work and more recently had been jobless for a year. The entire family was fed up with him.

"Don't be like that, Jamie," Layla implored. "He's trying to find a job. He really is."

"Yeah, OK."

Layla glanced at the floor for a brief moment, shame burning her face. "Can you still help us out this month? He says it will be the last time."

"I'm helping you and the kids, not him. I wish that you'd put him out, Layla. He's just another mouth to feed."

"I—I know," Layla stammered uncomfortably, "but it's not so simple when you have kids."

"It is simple. Mama and Daddy did fine with us after their divorce. The world didn't end when they separated."

"Yeah, but Daddy got married again, and Mama never did."

"So?"

"So maybe Paul is my only shot."

"Shot at what?"

"At being married. Most of my friends are single, and they keep telling me to think twice about divorcing Paul because at least I have a man."

"That's the stupidest advice that I've ever heard."

"Stupid to you, maybe, because you treat your job like it's a man."

Jamie gasped. "I do not!"

"Yes, you do, Jamie. And that's OK if it works for you, but I don't want to be single for the rest of my life like Mama."

Jamie waited for Layla to drop the last part of her statement: "or like you." But she kept that comment to herself. Still, the unspoken insult hung between them, and Layla tensely kept her eyes averted from Jamie's.

"Jamie! Long time no see, cuz!" One of their tub-size cousins, Franklin, appeared and picked Jamie up in a tight embrace as he spun her around in the air. "I want you to meet my fiancée, Hanna!" He set Jamie down and waved an arm in the air while his eyes scanned the room in several directions. "Hanna! Hanna! Girl, where'd you go off to? Hanna!"

Jamie rubbed her neck as though to cure a bout of whiplash. "I don't think that she can hear you over the music, Franklin. I'll meet her later."

14

"I met her already," Layla whispered, leaning in as Franklin continued to look over the crowd. "She's nice. I hope she's not just after his money."

"Me, too." Jamie was still smarting from Layla's unspoken marginalization, but decided to let it go.

Meanwhile, Franklin was visibly disappointed. "Yeah, I'll introduce you when I find her." His eyes continued to roam the room. "Just where the hell did she go?" Frustrated, he moved away in search of his bride-to-be.

Just then, Jamie spotted Paul, who resembled a pencil with a mustache, making his way over to her and Layla. At the sight of him, she nearly lost her appetite.

Jamie elbowed her sister. "Here comes Paul." A host of demeaning names for him spontaneously ran through her mind, while Layla pursed her lips and said nothing.

"What's up, Jamie?" Paul bobbed his head backward to accompany his lukewarm greeting.

"Hi. Where are the kids?"

"I told them to wait in the game room. I don't want them running around the house like some of these other kids. We've taught them better than that."

There were around twenty other children close in age to Sadie and Luke at the gathering. All of them were as well-mannered as expected, so Jamie didn't know what Paul was talking about. As usual, he had managed to annoy her within seconds of contact.

"Are you going to make their plates, Paul?" Layla looked anxious, having observed Jamie's agitation.

"Can't you make 'em? I've been watching the kids all day, and I'm tired."

"But I've been cooking all night. I'm sure that I'm more tired than you are."

"I seriously doubt that."

Layla stared incredulously at him for a long moment and then seemed to remember that Jamie was watching them closely with her arms crossed. Layla bit her lower lip and put her head down, defeated. "I'll make their plates."

"Would you make mine, too, and bring it to me on the patio?"

Layla defiantly met Paul's eyes and hissed through gritted teeth, "That I will not do." She then whipped around and marched off to join the other parents who were already preparing their children's dinner plates, leaving Jamie and Paul standing together.

Jamie contemptuously ignored him and held her breath. Of all the men on the planet, her sister had fallen for this irresponsible son of a—

"So how are things on the job, Jamie?"

"Fine. Everything's fine."

"Good. You know, maybe you could help Layla get on with your company. We could really use the money."

Jamie rolled her eyes and looked at him sideways. "Are you serious?"

"Of course I'm serious. We're tired of you supporting us. Speaking of which, did Layla talk to you about giving her a check today? We need to buy some groceries and pay the light bill."

"What about you getting a job so you can pay the bills yourself?"

"I'm working on it. You know that. But it's tough out there. And I'm not gonna be some kind of street sweeper or garbageman. I'm trying to get a real job that pays a lot of money, like a job with AT&T wiring phone lines in houses. I'd be good at that."

"Do you have any experience that qualifies you to do it?"

"No, but if they hire me, I will."

She exhaled a long breath and stared at the ceiling, asserting her entire will to remain calm. At that moment, she would have loved nothing more than to boot Paul right into the sunset that she had been admiring yesterday.

# CHAPTER 2

*A weed is but a flower that remains to be named.*

NOT LONG AFTER the Thanksgiving holidays, a blast of wintry temperatures beset the general Houston area, creating a crisp coolness outside that rivaled the comfort that Jamie found buried beneath her bedcovers. The abrupt weather change, coupled with the typical Monday-morning blues, incented her to doze longer than usual with Bear nestled against her, only the tip of her head exposed to the world beyond her cozy down comforter.

Seemingly from a distant universe, a bell began to ring incessantly. At first, the shrill sound was more like a faint jingle that could have originated from a mountaintop. But the grating cacophony soon punched through her deep slumber, forcing Jamie's resistant brain to acknowledge that the phone beside her bed was ringing and had to be answered.

Her hand flailed out in a blind search for the cordless phone located on the bedside table, clumsily fumbling around the top before finding the receiver and dragging it to her ear beneath the covers. "Hello," she mumbled groggily.

"Jamie? Hey, baby! Are you still asleep? I thought that you'd be up by now. It's almost seven." It was Ken, and he sounded like he had consumed a mug of pure caffeine.

At the news of the time, Jamie's eyes flew open as she threw back the covers and viewed the bright-red numbers on her electric clock. It was 6:55 a.m., and she had an eight o'clock meeting to attend at work.

"Oh my God!" She vaulted out of her bed in a panic. "Ken, I'm sorry, but I'll have to call you back later today when I get into the office. I'm running late and have to get there for an eight o'clock meeting."

"OK, but I wanted to talk to you about something before you leave."

"It'll have to wait. I can't believe that I overslept like this!" Jamie brushed Bear out of the bed and rapidly escorted him to the back door so that he could go out into the backyard while she took a shower.

"I just need a few minutes."

"Not right now, Ken. I'll call you from work, OK?" Jamie was breathless as she raced into her bathroom and turned on the water in the shower. "Gotta go!" She hung up on Ken before he could respond, hurriedly discarded her pajamas, and hopped into the shower.

Jamie frantically drove to work at breakneck speeds and then rushed with as much composure as possible to the

Radian conference room, where a handful of her vice-president colleagues were already seated for the early-morning meeting. For the most part, they were a stiff bunch, several years older than Jamie and beneficiaries of the good-old-boy network. From time to time, some employees like Jamie did manage to break through the iron ceiling and be promoted despite their lowly or nonexistent connections, but only when a job opened for which an exhaustive search failed to surface a well-known comrade to invite into the ranks. She knew all of these things well and accepted that fortune had smiled on her, but some small amount of resentment rolled indignantly around in her belly because her hard work and dedication should have been enough.

This morning's meeting was the VPs' weekly round-table with their boss, Tom Chase, the well-respected company president who looked old enough to be Jamie's great-grandfather. She adored Tom, but was worried that his confidence in her work might be suffering thanks to Jacob's confidential criticisms.

Speaking of the devil, Jacob ambled into the conference room along with a few others who accompanied Tom precisely at 8:00 a.m. Her eyes flickered past Tom's number-one crony, Randall Livingston, a fiftysomething loafer who seemed to draw a paycheck simply for showing up at work. No one knew what his job was, but they tolerated him because of his relationship with Tom. Unfortunately for Jamie, Randall had long been particularly interested in her despite all of her amiable rejections. And every once in a while, she got trapped sitting beside him in these meetings, but luck was with her this morning. Thankfully, there were no empty seats near Jamie, so she wouldn't be forced to endure Randall's come-ons. Nor would she be subjected to Jacob's small talk as if she wasn't smoldering inside. As Tom seated himself at the head of the twenty-foot-long table, Jacob and Randall lowered themselves into chairs directly across from Jamie. She was still separated from them by around four feet of table width, making almost any conversation between them and her impossible. Jacob winked, and Randall openly ogled Jamie, whose reaction was the equivalent of hardened concrete, before all attendees turned their attention to Tom.

"Good morning, everyone," Tom began, his voice calm and pleasant as he made eye contact with the twelve VPs around the table. "I hope that everyone enjoyed their Thanksgiving."

There were an assortment of agreeable responses and nods along with a few amicable glances exchanged between colleagues.

"Good, very good. I assume that you all have read the e-mail that my assistant forwarded to you last week about our new hire?"

This time, the collection of facial expressions was mixed, varying between entirely blank and fully informed.

"Am I to understand that some of you turned off your BlackBerrys during your vacations last week?" Tom was clearly amused, inviting lighthearted recriminations between colleagues. Like nearly all of her peers, Jamie had not read the e-mail and was surprised by the news. She pointedly kept her attention riveted on Tom, sensing that Jacob was trying to draw her eye from across the table.

"Well, for those of you who are behind with your e-mail," Tom continued, "suffice it to say that we've finally filled the product development VP role after a lengthy and grueling search. I feel good that we have landed a big fish in energy: a gentleman named Kenneth St. John, who is a recognized expert at alternative-energy solutions."

At the mention of Ken's name, Jamie emitted an audible, shocked gasp, drawing looks from the colleagues sitting near her. Immediately conscious of the unwanted attention, she tapped her throat with her fingertips and mouthed the words *dry throat*, which seemed to satisfy the curious onlookers. Everyone's attention was restored to Tom as Jamie began to shift uncomfortably in her chair.

"Since Kenneth is pretty well known in our industry, some of you may already be familiar with his work. For those of you who don't already know, he has a wealth of knowledge and achievements that have earned him a reputation as one of the foremost thinkers and innovators in energy. I recommend that you look him up on the Internet after you read the brief biography I've included in the e-mail that most you haven't read." Tom paused as a few people began whispering appreciatively, completely unaware of Jamie's mortification at the news that her long-distance lover was now local—and her coworker! How dare he take a job in Houston and, even worse, at *her company* without telling her! So that was why he had wanted to speak with her that morning.

With her lips drawn into an angry, stern line, Jamie blindly stared at Tom, her mind sifting through the information and its implications. She wondered if Ken had been crass enough to mention their relationship to Tom, the very thought of which set off a bomb within her that would have dwarfed a nuclear explosion. She again shifted in her chair, barely managing to conceal her rage from her peers.

"I can see that some of you already understand that we have much to be excited about now that Kenneth will be a key part of our team," Tom continued. "I believe that he will help to guide Radian into a very bright future, and I'm encouraging each of you to open up your minds to the new ideas that he will certainly bring to the table in the weeks and months to come. In the meantime, I've invited Kenneth to join us this morning and expect that he will do so shortly, once he has completed the fun-filled process of obtaining his security badge." He grinned slyly as everyone except Jamie chuckled. They all knew that Radian's security protocols were a royal pain. Meanwhile, Jamie remained trapped in her own isolated misery, doing her best to tame the fury and confusion that now gripped her entire being.

Before long, Tom's expression became more serious, and he waited for the room to quiet so that he could resume his comments. "As you all know, we have been faced with cutthroat competition since Congress deregulated the energy industry in 2002. Nearly every week since then, it seems that I hear about a new energy company or scheme starting up and offering lower rates than we do—a problem that is eroding our revenue and costing us customers that we've had for twenty years or more. Not only is it critical that we leverage Kenneth's proven talents to develop new products that promise to lure back and retain our customers, but we need to find creative ways to benchmark our prices against our competitors'." Tom gestured toward Jacob. "Jacob has talked to me about the possibility of using our employees as tools to obtain competitors' pricing agreements, and I think that it's a darn good idea."

Amid her deepening anger with Ken, this additional announcement kindled yet more confusion within Jamie, and she forced herself to better concentrate on Tom's update. If Jacob was getting accolades from Tom, why was Jacob trying to ruin her reputation and career? He was clearly on sure ground at the company. What could he possibly stand to gain by torpedoing her? Several eyes, including Jamie's, turned to acknowledge Jacob, who continued to watch Tom with transparent loyalty.

"This afternoon, I'd like for each of you to get buy-in from as many employees in your departments as possible to either switch their electric service from Radian to a competitor or, if they're already customers of our competitors, provide their pricing contracts. If we can get this information, then we can begin to take steps that are guaranteed to restore our edge and recuperate our income levels." Tom's instructions were met with silence as everyone evaluated them. "Any questions or thoughts?"

Barry Galeno, the VP of information technology, was the first to speak up. "Are we breaking any laws by obtaining the contracts this way?"

"I've already discussed that with Tom," Adam Lincoln, a self-proclaimed descendant of the sixteenth American president—and VP of the legal department—confidently replied. "Nothing comes to mind as being wrong with the plan, but I've tasked one of our legal associates to confirm that. We should know something by lunchtime today."

"If I may," Randall piped up, "I'd just like to say that I'm so thrilled that we're able to take such a creative approach to enhancing Radian's market appeal. I am continually awed by the staggering talent in this room." He displayed a full-toothed smile that no one except Jacob returned. Silence then lingered for a long moment before Tom spoke.

"Thank you, Randall. I'm sure that we all value the wealth of knowledge among us." Tom looked around the room. "I want you all to think of some incentives that we can offer to entice the employees to participate in this effort. You've got two days to present incentives to me that you yourselves would salivate over. How's that?"

The attendees nodded in unison as Jacob beamed, his large sea-blue eyes revealing his pleasure at having a moment to shine.

Just then, the door opened, and Tom's administrative assistant, Martha, ushered a tall, remarkably handsome African-American man into the room. "Tom, Mr. St. John can join y'all now."

At the sight of Ken, Jamie's anger resurged along with a monumental struggle for self-control. Ken, on the other hand, appeared to be completely relaxed and self-assured, as though all was right in the world.

Tom animatedly rose to approach Ken and to shake his hand. "You're just in time to listen in on the department updates." Tom turned back around to everyone else, meeting a thick silence with a jovial air. "Everyone, I'd like to introduce Kenneth St. John, our new product development vice president. As I said earlier, Kenneth is one of the industry experts on alternative-energy opportunities, and we are very fortunate that he was willing to leave Miami Power to contribute his knowledge to our organization."

Jamie's brain dwelled on the word *willing*. Ken had been *willing* to join Radian. For some reason, Tom was treating him like royalty.

"Now that you're here," Tom continued, "I can be honest and warn you that you've got your work cut out for you." He placed his palms on his plump belly and grinned.

"Thank you, Tom. I'm looking forward to the challenges." Ken was clearly undaunted by the caution. He curiously glanced around the room, his attention hovering on Jamie for a heartbeat longer than everyone else. Cringing inwardly and slumping down slightly, she desperately hoped that no one else had noticed.

Tom gestured to the room beyond the space that he and Ken shared near the door as Martha inconspicuously excused herself. "Kenneth, please have a seat anywhere you find an empty chair. Everyone, I'd like for each of you to introduce yourselves to Kenneth as we go around the table for your department updates. Please state your names and the departments you manage before launching into your laundry lists." Tom reseated himself as Ken confidently strode to a seat beside Jacob and sat down. The two men immediately shook hands, after which the VP to Ken's left politely tapped his shoulder and enthusiastically welcomed him to the team. Eventually, Ken looked across the table at Jamie, who regarded him with an expression that was barren of all recognition and friendliness. Upon observing her stoic disposition, Ken seemed somewhat bewildered but quickly recovered a more passive posture and readied his pen to begin jotting down notes on a writing pad that he had brought with him.

As the updates began and the first VP, Dale Taylor, announced himself, Jamie wondered how Ken had landed the job since he was definitely not part of the Radian crony network. Clearly, he had been extremely modest when describing his work to her when they were alone, as—based on Tom's comments earlier—Ken commanded a great deal of respect in the industry. But she shouldn't be surprised that she didn't know as much about him as she had thought, she decided, since the man had not bothered to mention being considered for a job at Radian. The idea of slapping him crossed her mind, and she contrived to maintain a poker face as Dale wrapped up his update. By the time he stopped talking, Jamie couldn't have repeated a single word of his presentation if her life had depended on it. And although she had come to the meeting prepared to provide some of her own updates, she now discovered that her normally adequate notes triggered no meaningful details in her memory. When it was her turn to speak, she drew a complete blank. So for the first time since being promoted to VP, Jamie's update was, "No comments today, guys. Thanks."

Embarrassed, she couldn't bear to look at Ken, but there was no way she could miss the critical, questioning gaze from Tom before he motioned for the next colleague to provide his updates, electing not to remark on Jamie's unusually poor showing.

As soon as Tom adjourned the meeting, Jamie fled the room, using the excuse of having an urgent personnel matter to attend to. Meanwhile, all of the other VPs stayed behind and quickly crowded around Ken to congratulate him on joining Radian.

Once safely back in her office with the door closed, Jamie paced and cursed Ken, brooding that she couldn't speak to—or, more correctly, yell at—him right now. It was impossible. She would have to wait since Tom would be virtually joined to Ken's hip for the entire day. Yet again, she cursed him for his deception. And she scolded herself for having failed to spot the signs that something was amiss.

Fully absorbed with her mania, Jamie was startled when someone knocked on the door and cracked it open.

"Hey, Jamie, are you joining everyone for lunch today?" It was Jacob, poking his head around the door. His timing couldn't have been worse, and her mood couldn't have been fouler.

She initially stood stock-still, not wanting to give away her toxic frame of mind. To buy a little time, she rigidly moved toward her desk and took a seat.

"What lunch?" She again concentrated on steeling herself.

"The lunch that Tom organized to welcome Kenneth to Radian. Didn't you see the meeting planner in your inbox?"

Jamie had not yet opened a single e-mail that morning. "Oh, that, yes. Of course, of course, I'll be there, but I may be running a little late. I, uh, I need to review some billing numbers." Her breath became more labored at the prospect of attending the lunch, and perspiration began to dampen her blouse beneath her suit coat.

"Postern product research?" To Jamie's chagrin, Jacob opened the door wider and stepped into the office.

"That, and some other items." She gave him the fakest smile in her repertoire, one that was frozen at the jawline and never reached her eyes. "But I'll definitely be at the lunch to welcome Ken to the team." She would be there because office politics wouldn't permit her to miss the gathering. It just wouldn't look good.

"Is it Ken or Kenneth? I don't recall anyone mentioning that we should call him Ken. Maybe I missed that."

"Oh, yeah, you're right," Jamie swiftly agreed, already anxious to end the topic and to get rid of him. "I'll have to ask him if he prefers Ken or Kenneth one of these days." She grabbed a sales report from the stack of papers on her desk and raised it to her eyes. "Listen, I need to get a lot done before lunch. I'll see you in a few hours."

"OK, my bad. Didn't mean to disturb you." He seemed disappointed at their conversation being cut short, but walked back outside of her office. "I'll see you later."

She deliberately chose not to respond, pretending that she had become engrossed with the report. But the moment he was out of sight, she closed her eyes, once again surrendering herself to the frustration and anger of having Ken working at the office. The only good news seemed to be that no one had any knowledge of their relationship. And Jamie had every intention of keeping it that way.

# CHAPTER 3

*Lovely roses. Truthful thorns.*

A MERE MONTH earlier, Jamie and Ken had ventured to a small wonderland of pleasure together in San Francisco. She had been looking forward to the trip and the complete change of pace since work had lately been a steady flow of difficulties. Jamie could hardly wait to take a break from it all, to exchange the drudgery for the ecstasy that Ken so ably supplied. Since meeting earlier that year, they had fallen into a pattern of picking cities that neither of them had ever visited and then meeting there to sightsee…among other things. The problem was that the other things—mainly their addiction to each other's bodies—had typically prevented them from seeing anything outside of their hotel rooms. But this time, things would be different. They were both committed to behaving like tourists in San Francisco. And they would do touristy things like go to see the Golden Gate Bridge, ride the cable cars, and visit the famous Wine Country.

But first, there was tonight, their inaugural evening in the city. As expected, Jamie's flight had arrived before his, and so she had rushed to their hotel to make preparations that she knew would please Ken as well as herself. After showering and applying cherry-scented lotion to her entire body, she donned only a sheer robe and waited.

He was so handsome, she thought when he eventually arrived and walked into the bedroom with his luggage. He had known that she would be there, and he smiled upon seeing her on the bed, just lying on her side with her head resting on the palm of her hand. Waiting. That night, his luggage and the clothes he had been wearing remained scattered near the bedroom entrance until morning broke. And as they did with each trip, they used each other to escape their individual lives and all of the toils that tugged at them. They were inseparable—literally. But their enchanted escape could last for only these few days together. Once Jamie returned to Houston, she would also be returned to her impenetrable fortress of work and all the related routines. That was the way she liked it. That was how she maintained such ironclad control of everything in her life.

Now Ken had encroached on Jamie's space and turned her fortress into a prison. So as soon as the clock struck five, Jamie thanked everything holy while preparing to leave the office. Since Ken had strutted into the conference room that morning, it had seemed that the quitting hour would never arrive and time had slowed down to the rate of dripping molasses. She could feel the heat, the steady burn of contempt boiling inside her. And she could hardly wait to retreat from the offense that had been paraded in her face all day.

If Ken had noticed her extreme consternation, he showed no signs, playfully testing her nerves earlier at lunch with their colleagues. She had nearly choked on her food when he had slyly commented that Jamie looked familiar to him and that perhaps they had met before. In an attempt to be polite, Jamie had acquiesced that it was possible, but she truly didn't recall, at which point Ken had wickedly assured her that they had indeed met, perhaps at an energy conference. Jamie had stopped chewing to shoot a poisonous glare in response, at which point he had nonchalantly moved on to a more harmless topic without any further surreptitious teasing. For the remainder of the gathering, Jamie had glowered at her plate, using her fork to stab the chicken cacciatore that had been served to everyone.

"The bastard!" Now at home, wearing a pink sweatshirt and matching jogging pants, Jamie was eager for Ken to arrive. She reminded herself that she had dated his type before, the egomaniac who couldn't see past his delusions of grandeur. Her last boyfriend, Dwight, had exhibited that quality, and she had dumbly tolerated it to keep him around. By the time they had broken up, she was just as sick of herself as she was of him. The final straw had been his demand that she choose between him and Bear. To his shock, Jamie had chosen Bear; to her shock, he had actually cut her loose.

Currently wired to the hilt, Jamie labored to keep herself distracted with housework, unable to simply be still and wait for the showdown with Ken, who had called to say that he would come by her home at around seven o'clock that evening. The time now was six thirty, and Jamie had just started loading laundry into the washing machine when she heard the doorbell ring, followed by Bear's excited yapping as he made a mad dash for the front door.

Jamie hastily dropped a handful of towels and hustled from the utility room down the long hallway that led to the front of the house. Upon opening the front door, her first impulse was to strangle the man who stood so confidently in her doorway, but she would've had to get through two dozen red roses to reach his neck. Nonplussed, Jamie scowled at the flowers.

"Hey, baby!" Ken grinned broadly and held out the roses. "I wanted you to have these. I thought it was the least I could do after the way I teased you at lunch today." As he had done then, he smirked like a little devil.

Jamie took a step back and opened the door wider without moving to accept the roses. "Come in." No hint of warmth or welcome crept into her voice. "Hurry up. It's cold outside."

He stepped through the doorway and leaned down to kiss her, but she quickly dodged his lips before closing the door behind him. Genuinely surprised, he carefully studied Jamie's face when she turned back around. "Are you mad at me?"

"Mad?" She placed her palm on her chest. "What would I be mad about, Ken?" Without waiting for his response, she started the trek back down the hallway, the destination this time being the sizable living room, where they could sit and talk. "Follow me."

"You're actually mad? But I was just joking around." He was still wearing his navy-blue business suit and black leather shoes, which echoed against the hardwood floor along with Bear's incessant barking behind her. Still badly underestimating the seriousness of the situation, he remarked, "So this is the infamous Bear and Château Dubois. Very nice house."

They had reached the living room, which was decorated with a mixture of multicolored artwork, unlit white candles, and an assortment of artificial plants. Jamie had chosen a color scheme composed of various earth tones with peach-colored accents that added a nice brightness to the room. It was a calming space, but Jamie's sentiments at the moment were exactly the opposite of calm. She gestured toward one of the beige sofas that faced the television, which was switched off.

"Thank you. Have a seat."

"What do you want me to do with these?" He again held out the roses.

"You can set them down right there in front of you." She pointed to a large, elegant coffee table made of hardwood and glass that was positioned within inches of his feet.

Clearly mystified by her cold treatment, Ken never-theless complied with Jamie's instructions as she seated herself in an armchair that had sufficient space for only one person. Bear immediately leapt onto her lap and leaned his small body against her chest.

Although bewildered, Ken seemed to have finally com-prehended that he was in deep trouble with Jamie. After set-ting down the roses, he took a seat on the large sofa that she had pointed out across from her chair, brought his palms together, and leaned forward. "What's wrong, Jamie?"

She wasted no time getting right to the point. "Everything. Everything is wrong. I cannot believe you accepted a job at Radian and moved to Houston without talking to me first. Why would you do that?"

"Because I got the job offer of a lifetime. They came to me. Apparently, Tom has been trying to fill the position for several months, and he thought about hiring me after we met at the energy conference in Chicago."

"You mean that you've been in talks with Tom ever since we met?" Jamie was astounded by this revelation.

"Actually, yes, I have. And he met all of my terms. There was no way I could turn him down." Ken seemed unruffled as Jamie's agitation spiked. "What's the prob-lem? I thought that you'd be happy about all of this."

"Why should I be happy?"

"Because I'm here now, baby. We don't have to fly across the country to see each other anymore. No more trips and hotels."

"I happened to like the trips and hotels, Ken. I liked everything exactly as it was."

"Nah! I don't believe that." Ken shook his head dismissively. "You didn't like the distance between us. We hardly saw each other."

"That's right. We hardly saw each other, and that was perfect."

"Jamie, you're not making any sense. Are you saying that you don't want to see me?"

"Not every day, no."

Ken's degree of discomfiture visibly rose. "Why not?"

"Because I just don't want to."

Ken slid back deeper into the sofa and silently looked at Jamie before asking, "Are you seeing someone else?"

"No."

"Then what's the problem?"

"The problem is that I like my space. And you have just invaded it without my permission."

"OK, I see. I see." He nodded his head curtly. "So I'm guessing that you don't ever want to get married since you don't like having men in your space on a regular basis."

"Why? Are you implying that you'd like to marry me?" Jamie's tone had turned sarcastic.

"I don't know. Maybe I had thought that there was a possibility. Eventually. Someday."

Jamie sneered incredulously. "I can count with my fingers and toes the number of times I've heard that line. I'm not some twentysomething, desperate disaster of a woman who hangs on your every word. And I don't need you or any other man to complete me. You shouldn't flatter yourself that way."

"I know that you're successful, Jamie, but even a successful woman needs love."

"So now you love me?" She raised a skeptical eyebrow.

Ken abruptly stood up and looked down at her. "I don't like this side of you. You sound like a bitter old woman."

"Hey, I'm just trying to make sure I understand why I'm supposed to be so grateful that you moved to Houston and took a job at Radian."

He merely looked at her.

"I see what's going on, Ken, and I'm not stupid enough to think that I was a major factor in your decision to come here. You were offered a plum job, and you took it. Congratulations. You got what you wanted."

"That's not all that I wanted."

"Sure it was. If I had been important to your plans, you would've told me about them."

"Jamie, I—" Ken struggled, clearly overcome with anger as well. He grunted a few times, almost saying something, but then stopping himself as though searching for the right words. Before he could find them, the phone rang.

Jamie's head jerked sideways toward the sound. Although the cordless phone was conveniently within reach on a side table near her chair, she thought about ignoring the call. But then she decided to check the caller ID and saw that it was Layla. Jamie sighed heavily and pressed a button to accept the call while Ken remained still, glaring at her.

"Hey, Layla," Jamie sourly greeted her sister and heard stifled sniffles in response. "Layla? Are you there?"

After a few more sniffles, "Yes, I'm here," Layla croaked between sobs.

"What's wrong?" A range of possible answers raced through Jamie's mind as she imagined the worst. For the moment, she completely forgot that Ken was standing near her.

"Can I come over with the kids? We need a place to stay tonight, and I don't want to go to Mama's house."

"Of course you can stay here. You all can stay as long as you need to. But what's wrong?"

Jamie could hear her sister's choppy breathing. "Paul and I had another fight, and I just can't be under the same roof with him tonight. I hate the sight of him!"

"OK, come on over with the kids, and we'll talk about it when you get here." It wasn't the first time that Layla had needed a place to go following an argument with Paul. Jamie was relieved that the problem was only an argument.

"OK, we'll be there in thirty minutes. We're already in the car."

"That's fine. I'll see you soon."

"Wait! Jamie?"

"Yes?"

"Thank you."

"You're welcome. Drive safely." Jamie ended the call and looked at Ken, suddenly feeling exhausted by all of the day's drama.

"Is Layla OK?" Ken had never met Jamie's family, but he'd heard all about them from her. Like Jamie, he seemed to have sobered, the phone interruption having doused the fire in both of them.

"Yeah, she and Paul just had another argument." Jamie stood up and set Bear down. "She's going to spend the night here with the kids."

"OK, well…" He continued to gaze at Jamie, seeming uncertain of whether he should say whatever had crossed his mind during Jamie's call with Layla. "I, uh—" he struggled before glancing at his feet and giving up. "I'm going to leave." He stuffed his hands in his pockets and looked at Jamie, who said nothing. "Maybe we can finish talking about this later."

"I honestly don't have anything else to say." Jamie's voice sounded peculiar to her own ears as the mental fatigue she felt began to weigh down her shoulders.

He nodded curtly, his lips tightening before he released a long, heavy breath. "Jamie, I think I need to remind you that I'm not your enemy. You don't need to declare war on me just because I didn't tell you about the job at Radian. I only have the best intentions toward you. I hope that you believe that."

The sincerity of his words was laid bare in his eyes as he waited in vain for Jamie to respond. But she only looked at him, unsure of what she thought or felt. Finally, Ken resignedly turned and strode quickly to the front door as Jamie watched him let himself out. While she didn't know how she felt about Ken, she was definitely glad that he was gone.

She glanced at the roses that he had brought, unsure of what to do with them. Like Ken, they were an invasion of her territory, and her first impulse was to throw them into the garbage. But a part of her felt guilty about disposing of them while they were still so vibrant. Perhaps she would simply put the roses in the kitchen and out of her sight. That felt like the better option. Just get them out of her sight until they died, as they surely would. As all flowers did. Before picking up the roses, she pressed the fleshy part of one of her fingertips gently against a thorn. The thorn easily won the test of fortitude.

When Layla arrived with her kids, it was obvious that she had been crying. Her eyes were swollen, and the skin around them was rubbed to an irritated red color. Rather than discuss the argument with Paul in front of Luke and Sadie, the two sisters went about feeding and bathing the children before putting them to bed in one of Jamie's guest bedrooms.

Once they were tucked in, Jamie and Layla reclined together at opposite corners of Jamie's largest living room sofa under a king-size blanket that Jamie had collected from a linen closet. It was approaching 10:00 p.m., all of the curtains were drawn tightly, and the only sound in the house was the television as Jamie and Layla looked at each other.

"So what did you and Paul argue about this time?" Jamie pulled her end of the blanket up over her neck as Bear curled up on her stomach and began licking one of his paws on top of the cover.

"The same stuff that we always argue about." The dark circles under Layla's eyes were worse than they had been at Thanksgiving. She looked like she could sleep for at least a week. "I told him that he needs to get a job because we can't keep relying on you for money every month."

"Oh. I'm sure that he's tired of you saying that."

"Not tired enough. He started talking about the application that he submitted to AT&T and how he's waiting for them to call him for an interview. And while he's waiting, he's living off of me and my family! So I decided to take matters into my own hands. I brought home a Walmart job application today for him to fill out." Layla already worked at Walmart for minimum wage as a cashier.

"Really?" Jamie sat up straighter.

"Yes, really! He likes to work out, so I figured that he can get paid to work out. He can get a job lifting heavy boxes and stocking shelves at Walmart. There's nothing wrong with that. And while he's stocking shelves, he can keep on waiting for AT&T to call him."

At this, Jamie burst into laughter, soon being joined by Layla despite the seriousness of the problem. "It was a good idea," Jamie eventually lamented once their laughter had settled down, "but Paul will never go for it."

"I know, which is why I've asked him to move out."

Jamie's eyes widened. "You did? When? Today?"

"Yeah." Layla shrank further beneath the blanket and clutched it closer to her body. "I just can't take it anymore. And I can't have my children growing up thinking that it's normal for a grown man to live off of a woman. He's setting the wrong example for them while I work my fingers to the bone to keep a roof over our heads. Not to mention the fact that we're acting like beggars every month when the light bill comes due and we don't have the money." Unbidden tears suddenly erupted from Layla's eyes and flowed down her cheeks. "I feel so bad that we've burdened you like that. And I'm ashamed of him. I don't understand how he can even look people in the eye."

"It's all right, Layla. I'm here for you and the kids. I wouldn't help if it was a problem for me."

"And I appreciate that, Jamie, but you're not an ATM. You shouldn't be treated as if you are."

Jamie wasn't sure of what to say, so she remained silent for a few moments. Layla had married Paul despite their family's warnings, stubbornly asserting that he would turn out to be her knight in shining armor and eventually earn wealth beyond everyone's belief. As it was, they had been living on the verge of abject poverty.

Sensitive to her sister's despair, Jamie finally asked in a near whisper, "So is he going to move out?"

"Of course not. Where would he go?" Layla rubbed away the tears that were still rolling down her face. "Nobody in his family is willing to let him live off of them the way he's been living off of us."

Again at a loss for how to respond, Jamie was silent. It was difficult to watch her sister struggle.

"I've been thinking a lot about Grandma lately." Layla now sat up straighter, folded her legs, and wrapped her arms around them as she spoke, still sniffling and obviously miserable. "You remember how much she loved Grandpa despite how badly he treated her?"

Jamie nodded silently.

"He never loved her the way she loved him. He disappeared on their wedding night, he cheated on her the whole time they were married, but she never left. Why? Why did she allow herself to be treated that way?"

"You know why. She loved him too much to leave. And she didn't believe in divorce." The sisters had heard fragments of their grandmother's story over the years, long after she had died.

"She should've left." Layla closed her eyes. "She should've said to herself that she could do better and that she deserved better."

"I know. She was such a good woman. And she really loved us."

"Yes, she did. But she didn't love herself enough to get out."

"Things were different back then. She made decisions that she thought were best for herself and her children. We can't fault her for that."

"I don't fault her, Jamie." Layla met her sister's eyes, and Jamie saw a gleam of conviction that she had not seen before. "But I'm not going to be like her. I'm not going to stay with a man who treats me like a maid or a doormat. Paul has been holding me down and pushing me down for long enough. And I will not take it anymore."

Jamie was blown away by this seismic shift in Layla's demeanor. "Sounds like you've been thinking about this for a long time."

"I have been. I'm tired, Jamie. Damned tired. And I should be. I've been carrying this man on my back ever since we got married, and he seems content to stay there. But his free ride is over. What kind of man refuses a job when he doesn't have one? I'll tell you what kind. A sorry one. One who thinks that he's already getting everything he wants without having to work. A man who sees nothing wrong with using other people. He's only thinking about himself, and I can't stay with a man like him. I will not live like Grandma did. I don't love Paul enough to let him demean me until I'm dead."

"I understand, Layla. I really do. And I'll do everything I can to support you."

"You've already done so much that I hate to ask for more."

"You're not asking. I'm offering. I want to help you. Just tell me what you need."

Layla cast her eyes downward. "I need a place to stay with the kids." She again looked at Jamie. "Just until I can get on my feet and find a new place of my own."

Jamie didn't hesitate. "Done. You can stay here for as long as you need to."

"Really? You'd be OK with that?" Layla exhaled with obvious relief.

"Of course! You're my sister. And I've got this big ole house with all this space. There's plenty of room for us all." Jamie smiled reassuringly.

"Thank you, Jamie." Layla stood up, crossed the small distance between them, and hugged Jamie tightly.

"You're welcome. You know that I have your back."

"Thank you, Jamie," Layla repeated. "I don't know what I'd do without you." After a few moments, Layla pulled away. "I just feel so stupid. I've really made a mess of my life."

"Yeah, well, I haven't done much better." Jamie sank back down beneath the blanket as Layla returned to her own spot at the other end of the sofa. "I've gone out with a billion men and never come across that one jewel that everyone said was out there waiting for me."

Layla settled back in under the blanket and looked at Jamie. "It sounds so pitiful when you put it that way." They were silent for a few moments as they each reflected on their lives before Layla eventually spoke again. "But you're not really alone. You have Ken."

"Oh brother." Jamie rolled her eyes. "No, I don't have Ken."

"Well, you've got somebody. Who gave you the flowers that I saw in the kitchen?" Now Layla had a different, mischievous look in her eyes.

Jamie adjusted her position as Bear leapt onto the floor. She didn't want to answer Layla's question.

"Well?"

"Well what?" Jamie coyly dodged.

"Who gave you the flowers?"

Jamie heaved a long sigh. "Ken."

"I knew it!" Layla threw a pillow at Jamie. "Why didn't you tell me how serious things were getting?"

"What makes you think we're getting serious?"

"Come on, Jamie! You know that men only send flowers to women they love."

"Says who?"

"Says…I don't know. History."

"Not my history. Nearly every man I've ever dated has brought me flowers. And where are they now? They're all gone. Most of them are married to other women, and I'll bet you that they didn't bother getting any flowers for them. There's no need to bring flowers to a woman who will only settle for a ring. Flowers are just a trick, a decoy."

"You're being ridiculous. So it didn't work out with those guys, but maybe it will work out with Ken. Maybe he's the one." Despite her own disappointing circumstances, Layla remained a hopeless romantic.

"He's not the one."

"How do you know?"

"Because I just know, OK?"

Layla silently stared at Jamie. "He scares you, doesn't he?"

"No, of course not. He pisses me off."

"What's he done to piss you off? All I ever hear about are fancy hotels and sexathons."

"He's got some selfish qualities that I don't like. He only thinks about himself."

"Can you give me an example?"

Jamie had grown exasperated with the conversation. "He's just—he's too young for me. And he cares more about his job than he does about what I may want."

"You mean that he's like you?"

"No, he's not like me!"

"Sounds like he is to me."

"I just said that he's too young for me. He's not as mature and stable as the men my age are."

"And to what men are you referring?" Layla was now goading Jamie.

"He's just not my type, Layla. We've talked about this."

"I know we have. And I've just let you babble on and on about Ken being your secret toy as if that's all it actually was. But I've never believed it—not for one minute."

"Then you don't know me as well as you think. I don't have time for a relationship right now. And I certainly would never get serious about Ken."

"Why not, Jamie? I still don't understand what your problem is. So he's a little younger than you. So what?"

Jamie had not intended to share the most recent developments with Layla tonight, but she finally blurted, "He just took a job at Radian."

"No!" Layla nearly leapt off the couch. "He's working from Florida?"

"He moved to Houston. I just found out today."

Layla clapped both of her hands over her mouth. "Oh my God! You know what that means, don't you?"

"Yeah. It means that he's a selfish jerk like I've been telling you."

Layla reached across and slapped Jamie's arm.

"Ow! Why'd you do that?"

"Because you're being stupid. He moved here because he wants to marry you, you dummy!"

"Ken does not want to marry me any more than I want to marry him. He moved here because he was offered a great job, and he didn't care about how I would feel about him working at the same company."

"Uh-huh, OK." Layla relaxed against the sofa once more. The mischievous glint had returned to her eyes.

"Why are you looking at me like that?"

"Because I think that I'm right and you're wrong."

Jamie glanced at her feet and shook her head. "This is a disaster. I can't date someone who I work with. Been there, done that."

"You're talking about Ellis?" Ellis had been Jamie's coworker at a different company several years ago. When things had gone south, she'd been forced to find another job to escape him, the office rumor mill, and the potential damage to her promotion opportunities. He was the catalyst for her landing at Radian.

"Uh-huh. I learned the hard way to keep my personal life separate from my professional life."

"I remember." Layla's mood now swung dramatically downward. "Maybe things will be different this time with Ken."

Jamie said nothing as she searched herself for any reason to bother any further with Ken. Layla seemed to have read Jamie's thoughts.

"Why don't you think about it for a while? Don't do anything hasty that you might regret later."

"I don't know." Jamie frowned. "Everything was so simple and fun. Now it's complicated and inconvenient."

"Life is like that sometimes."

"Not the life I want." Mentally drained, Jamie exhaled long and hard. "I've had enough complications to last me a lifetime."

Layla nodded sympathetically. "You and me both. To tell you the truth, I think I need to be more like you and just cut men loose as soon as they give me a reason to question anything about them."

Layla's comment was completely at odds with the perspective she had expressed at Thanksgiving. "I thought that you didn't want to be like me," Jamie said.

Layla looked confused. "I've never said that."

"You implied it at Thanksgiving when you said that I treat my job like a man and you don't want to be single for the rest of your life."

"Single like Mama, not you."

"What's the difference?"

Once again, Layla just looked at Jamie. They held each other's eyes until Layla finally dropped hers to her lap. "It's not about you or Mama. It's about me. It's been really hard to imagine a life without Paul. We've been together since high school. I've never been alone like you and Mama. And maybe that's the problem. I've been scared to even try to stand on my own two feet."

"I understand, Layla," Jamie attempted to console her. "I never thought about being alone until Dwight and I broke up. I guess I was just ready for a break from the chaos. And after a while, I realized that it wasn't so bad."

"But now you have Ken."

"For the last time, I do not have Ken." Jamie was plainly petulant.

"All right, if you say so." Layla pulled the blanket closer around her as Jamie rose from the sofa.

"I'm going to hit the sack. I'll see you in the morning." Jamie began walking toward her bedroom.

"OK. Don't forget that I have to work tomorrow evening and I'll be back pretty late."

"Is Mama keeping the kids?"

"Yeah, since I got the late shift again." Layla's unpredictable work schedule was yet another inconvenience to everyone in the family. Since Paul considered feeding and putting the kids to bed a woman's work, he burdened everyone else by refusing to perform such menial tasks whenever Layla had to work late hours. "I'll probably go to bed in a few minutes."

"All right. Good night, then."

"Good night. And Jamie?"

Jamie turned back to look at Layla. "Huh?"

"Thanks again. I really do appreciate what you're doing for us."

"You would do the same for me." Jamie continued to her room, soon closing the door behind her. Unlike Layla, she was glad to finally be alone.

# CHAPTER 4

*And what when the petals inevitably wilt?*

THE NEXT MORNING, Jamie arrived at the office at the crack of dawn, resolved to focus on her work instead of the distraction that Ken had created. With a hot mug of coffee in hand, she tuned everything else out—every distressing thought—and threw herself into digging out of an e-mail pileup. She was halfway out of the hole shortly before 8:00 a.m. when her phone rang, signaling that the normal morning scramble was starting. She pressed the speaker button to take the call without checking the caller ID.

"Jamie Dubois," she announced herself while continuing to scan the e-mail she had begun to read.

"Good morning, Jamie. How are you doing?" It was Tom's administrative assistant, Martha.

"Hi, Martha. I'm good. How are you doing?" Jamie immediately stopped reading the e-mail and redirected her attention to the call, a small knot of anxiety already forming in her stomach.

"I'm fine. Thank you for asking."

"Good, I'm glad to hear it. What can I do for you?"

"I'm calling to set up a meeting with you and Tom this morning. He'd like for you to stop by in around thirty minutes, but it looks like your calendar is booked for most of the day."

"Yes, that's correct. I have a few meetings scheduled, but I've also blocked off some time to review several reports that my team has drafted." As she spoke, Jamie used her mouse to select the icon that would bring up her calendar on her computer screen, already knowing that she had planned to meet with Julia, one of the directors on her team, to discuss staffing issues at eight thirty. Meanwhile, her anxiety was fast converting into a queasiness that bordered on nausea. She had already guessed what Tom wanted to discuss.

"Are you able to move anything around so that you can meet with Tom this morning?" Although framed as a request, Jamie understood that Martha had actually issued a command on Tom's behalf.

"Yes, I'll do that right now." She selected the eight-thirty meeting on her calendar and checked Julia's calendar for a different time that worked for them both.

"Great, so then eight thirty will work?"

"Yep, eight thirty is good." She mechanically went through the motions of updating the meeting with Julia to a later time as a fearful lump formed in her throat and dispersed itself throughout her body.

"OK, I'll set it up right now. Thanks!"

When Jamie shut off the speaker, she realized that her hand was trembling. She was terrified about what Tom might be planning to say, particularly since she still had no idea why Jacob had told him that she was performing poorly. Unfortunately, the information she did have was all supposition, so she had had no choice but to lay in waiting, hoping that the accusation would prove inaccurate without her mounting a self-defense. But Tom's spontaneous meeting request could only mean that he had finally decided to discuss the issues that Jacob had alleged.

Jamie furtively glanced at the small clock at the bottom of her computer screen: 8:02. She had around twenty minutes to get herself together and to still her mind. For the millionth time in the past week, she searched her memory for anything that could possibly be the root cause of the supposed performance issue, and for the millionth time, she came up with nothing. She would have to wait to hear what Tom had to say and do everything in her power to reassure him that his concerns were completely unfounded.

As she nervously evaluated how to handle the meeting with Tom, a group of incoming employees waved their greetings as they passed by her open door. She wryly acknowledged them while wishing that she could sink right into the floor.

Suffering from a heightened state of anxiety, Jamie trudged to Tom's office for their meeting and lightly rapped her knuckles on his solid-wood door before entering. His office was at least twice the size of hers and filled with various photos of his wife, their three grown children, and their grandchildren.

"Hi, Tom." She tried to sound unconcerned, confident—anything other than the way she was actually feeling.

"Ah, good morning, Jamie." He looked up with a more chipper expression than Jamie had expected, and she felt a pang of hope. "Would you mind closing the door, please? I'd like to have a private conversation with you."

Not a good sign. Her heart again sank, this time farther down to her knees, as she turned back around to close the door. She then took a seat near Tom's desk and clasped her hands in her lap out of his view.

"Thank you for coming on such short notice, Jamie. I apologize if I inconvenienced you, but I thought that the subject we need to discuss is too important to wait." He rested his forearms on his desk and looked at her with a pleasant expression.

Although Jamie had always known that Tom genuinely liked her, his amiable demeanor was contrary to what she would expect if he were planning to have a tough conversation with her. Like a pulley with a disintegrating line, Jamie's emotions continued to rise and fall erratically as she tried to predict Tom's reasons for calling the last-minute meeting.

"No problem, Tom. I knew that this must be an urgent meeting, so I moved a few other things around."

"Yes, and I appreciate your doing that for me." Tom had always been a gracious man. It was one of the many qualities that Jamie liked about him. He now sat back in his chair, making himself more comfortable and removing his eyeglasses. "I'd like to talk to you about Kenneth."

Shocked by the mention of Ken's name, Jamie braced herself as a mixture of anger and apprehension replaced the nervousness and fear that had consumed her for nearly thirty minutes. Ken must have told Tom about them! Not trusting herself to speak at the moment, she only looked at Tom with her most practiced indifferent expression. Meanwhile, her leg had begun to twitch beneath the desktop.

"I need to ensure that Kenneth hits the ground running here, and I think that you and your team can be instrumental to making that happen."

Once again, Jamie was surprised, and a tidal wave of relief began to wash over her as she mentally processed Tom's politely framed directive. "Oh, sure, we're certainly happy to do whatever we can."

Tom paused to look more closely at Jamie and tilted his head curiously. "Jamie, are you OK this morning? You seem to be a little on edge."

"No, I'm fine. Really." She exhaled a quick breath to help compose herself. "Is there anything specific that you'd like for my team to do to help Ken?"

"Is it Ken or Kenneth? I guess that you've had a chance to speak with him?"

As she had when speaking with Jacob yesterday, Jamie had forgotten to use Ken's full first name and kicked herself. She didn't want to suggest any level of familiarity with the man, but before she could correct her oversight, Tom continued.

"That's good because you two will be spending a lot of time together over the next few weeks. I want you, Ivan, Julia, and Sam to set up quick daily meetings with Kenneth to go over the performance trends of all of our product offerings. And not just the products in our current portfolio. I'd like for you to also talk about the products that we retired before Alfredo left the company." Alfredo was Ken's predecessor.

It was a curious request, but Jamie wasn't inclined to inquire about why the retired products should be included as topics with Ken. For now, she was just glad that her job wasn't in jeopardy, even if it meant having to spend more time with Ken than she preferred.

"We will definitely be sure to do that. I'll ask Hyo to set up the meetings today." Relieved, she stood up to leave, assuming that Tom had completed his agenda.

"Jamie, before you go, there's just one more thing."

"OK." She sat back down, abruptly feeling the queasiness return.

"I'd like to know how you're feeling about your workload. I'm a little concerned that I may have saddled you with too much in the last few months."

There it was. The other shoe had finally dropped. Jamie struggled to remain calm.

"No, I don't think so. We have everything under control."

"You seemed to be a little out of sorts at the meeting yesterday morning. I thought that maybe it was because of all of the projects that you're involved with. Perhaps we should look at opportunities to move some of that work to other groups that can absorb it."

"Tom, I don't think that that's necessary. Yesterday wasn't one of my best days, and I apologize for that, but I haven't heard any concerns or complaints that anyone on my team needs relief. And I certainly don't feel overwhelmed. Was something overlooked that I'm not aware of?" Jamie fought back the panic that was building within her.

"*Overlooked* isn't the right word." Tom absently placed the end of one of his eyeglass stems between his front teeth. "Maybe the better word is *uncover*."

"Uncover what?"

"The reason why we're not meeting our long-term revenue projections on the Postern product. I was talking to Jacob a couple of weeks ago, and I understand that his sales team is beating the projected customer-entry expectations, but for some reason, we're missing the revenue targets."

"Yes, they are signing up a significant number of both new and existing customers, which my team evaluates each month. However, an average of fifty percent of those customers choose to drop the product after the third month. And seventy-five percent of the customers who drop the product are also switching their service away from Radian, which is compounding the problem. Ivan has already discussed all of this with Jacob's team."

"That's a very troubling trend. Who did Ivan talk to about the problem?"

"I don't recall exactly, but he spoke with someone around three weeks ago, I think."

"Hmm…" Tom chewed on the end of his eyeglass stem. "Maybe this information didn't reach Jacob. Any idea yet why the customers are dropping out?"

"Not yet. We're looking into potential weaknesses in the script that customer service agents use to describe the product to prospective customers. Maybe the script needs to be revised and clarified so that customers better understand how the rates incrementally increase. We're also planning to research some other potential issues, like whether certain customers had unusual spikes in their energy usage after signing up." Jamie's natural confidence reasserted itself as she explained her team's research strategy.

"Good, good. I don't remember any updates on this problem in the weekly meetings."

"That's definitely my fault. I was trying to nail down the root cause before bringing it up in that forum." Jamie had actually planned to mention the research plans in yesterday's inopportune meeting, but she couldn't admit the truth to Tom under these circumstances.

"I see. And I understand. But in light of the amount of money we're losing, your team's investigation needs to be swift so that we can put a solution into place as soon as possible. In our business, three weeks is a long time to know about a problem without solving it."

"I agree, and I assure you that we're on top of it. I'll ask Ivan if we can speed up the research. I'm sure it's not a problem." She would also assign any additional resources that Ivan deemed necessary to identifying the core issue as quickly as possible. He was one of her leading performers, and she had a great deal of confidence in him.

"Very well. If you and Ivan could give me a delivery ETA sometime this week, I'd be eternally grateful."

Jamie nodded confidently. "We'll do that." Before standing up again to leave, she asked, "Is there anything else?"

"No, that's it for now." He seemed curiously reserved, again aggravating Jamie's unsettled feelings, although at least the queasiness was gone.

"All right." She stood up and began walking toward the door. "I'll speak to Ivan as soon as I get back to my office." She practically clutched the doorknob as she opened the door.

"Sounds good, Jamie. Thanks for stopping by." Tom had put his glasses back on and turned his attention to his computer screen.

Set free from the chamber of looming doom, Jamie gave her best attempt at a leisurely stroll past Martha's desk. Upon rounding the corner, though, she picked up the pace with a sense of urgency, making a beeline to see Ivan, Julia, and Sam to request that they all be in her office at nine thirty sharp. After days on end with no understanding of why Jacob had criticized her job performance to Tom, she finally had had the problem outlined to her and harbored no misgivings that she absolutely must mount her defense as quickly as humanly possible to fully restore Tom's confidence in her. And if her suspicions were correct, her team's findings would somehow lead right back to Jacob instead of to her.

Four weeks earlier on their first night in San Francisco, Jamie and Ken had enjoyed their usual binge lovemaking, basking in the sensual motion of their bodies moving together until sleep descended upon them. As the curtains were drawn, very little sunlight filtered into their room, but the feeling of time stealing their moments eventually awakened Jamie, who then nudged Ken. They must see the city, they rapidly recommitted to each other. They must tour San Francisco like normal people did. But before embarking on their exploits, they also had to get breakfast like normal people did. And so they showered and dressed, barely repressing their mutual preference to remain in their room rather than saunter to a corner booth in the hotel dining area.

"How's Layla doing these days?" Ken gazed at Jamie with renewed hunger that had nothing to do with food. She told herself to resist his magnetism or else another trip would go down as a very expensive orgy. But he was making it hard for her. She sipped her water.

"She's hanging in there, although I don't know how."

"You know what they say—love is blind."

"They should say that love is demented."

"Don't be so hard on her. She knows that she's in a bad situation."

"I don't know what she knows since she won't leave Paul." The waiter approached and took their order. Then Jamie unfolded her table napkin and spread it neatly across her lap before continuing with her thoughts. "Sometimes I can't believe that Layla and I have the same two parents."

"I know what you mean. I think the same thing about Marvin sometimes."

Jamie smiled and drank more water. "What's he been up to?"

"The same ole, same ole, plowing through women like some kind of bulldozer. He doesn't care what kind of women either. He just wants to get as many into bed as he can."

"Why? I've never understood men who think that way."

"Because he thinks it's fun. And women let him do it, so he's going to do it." Ken often shared the unvarnished male perspective with Jamie during their conversations.

"But you'd think that he'd get bored with that. And what about all the diseases people have nowadays?"

He shrugged and glanced around the restaurant. "He doesn't care. I've tried to warn him. He's already got one kid he didn't plan on. But you can't tell him anything. The boy is stubborn."

"If he's not careful, he's going to have another kid."

"Or mess around with the wrong woman and get shot."

"You really think that?"

"Yeah, there's some crazy women out there."

"There's some crazy men, too."

"I know." Ken frowned and looked at Jamie. "I could never live like Marvin. He's running through a field of land mines as if none of them can blow up."

"So you don't plow through women?"

"No. I did back in the day, but I stopped because I didn't like hurting women. They got so attached, and I just wasn't looking for that. I wanted my freedom. And when one of Marvin's flings got pregnant, I knew I had to slow down 'cause I'm not trying to be somebody's baby daddy."

Jamie laughed at his use of the common colloquialism.

"I'm serious. Not this man." He haughtily shook his head as Jamie looked on fondly, still humored. If even half of what he had said was true, Ken would be a good husband to someone when he was ready to settle down. And it seemed that his future wife would be a very lucky woman. As for Jamie, settling down was nowhere on her radar.

Jamie sat in her office, her thoughts entirely centered on the job she was being paid to do.

"Hey, Jamie, do you have a sec?"

Immediately recognizing the voice, she winced. Ken had entered while she read one of the last outstanding e-mails that required her response. The morning had started with a flurry of activities aimed at brainstorming a different strategy to tackle the Postern product research, and now she was finally catching up on her normal workload. Somewhat deflated by his presence in her space, she couldn't help sighing when she looked up in response to the interruption. She had to be professional even though she would have liked nothing more than for him to disappear.

"Yes, what's up?" Her tone was completely impersonal.

"Do you mind if I close the door?" He seemed uneasy.

"This really isn't a good time, Ken." Again, she detested the fact that he was now her coworker. He was already cutting off her oxygen.

"I just need a few minutes, if that's OK."

He was so humble that she felt guilty about heeding her better judgment to kick him out. "Sure, OK."

Ken closed the door and then drew closer to Jamie's desk. She noticed that he had a few sheets of paper in his hands. "First, I want to apologize for not telling you about the job offer here. It never occurred to me that you would be so upset. I thought about everything you said yesterday, and I tried to put myself in your shoes and think about how I would feel if you had moved to Miami and joined my company. Personally, I think that I would have been extremely flattered." He grinned sheepishly. "But I understand that you see things differently, and I respect that. I want to make things right between us, Jamie. How can I do that?"

"That's easy. You can quit and get a job somewhere else. But I'll bet that you're not going to do that. You're not that sorry, are you?"

Ken balked at the suggestion. "This job is the best chance I've ever had to make a really big mark in the industry. If I'm successful here, I'll be set for life. I'll be able to go anywhere I want to go."

"That's interesting because just yesterday you said that I was the reason that you had come here."

"And that is true. You are one of the reasons." Ken walked a little closer to her desk. "Look, you're angry right now. I get it. You've made your point. But why don't you try to see things from my point of view? This job could bring us closer and change the whole trajectory of my career at the same time."

"And that's what it's all about—you," Jamie spat.

"And you."

"Don't insult my intelligence. You've got me mistaken for a dumb cluck." Ken's jaw literally dropped at Jamie's response. Increasingly agitated, she artlessly changed the subject, again glancing at the papers in his hands. "Did you need to discuss anything work-related? What are those documents you brought with you?"

Ken didn't seem ready to move on, but he took the hint and switched gears to polished professionalism. "Right, yes, I want to talk about these Postern product reports that I printed out." He walked around Jamie's desk and spread the reports out before her. Since her team had distributed the reports, she already knew them quite well. Ken pointed to the prior three months' activities reflected on all three pages. "Do you have any information about why the product performance declined so sharply in the last quarter? I've been looking for any materials that explain it, but maybe I'm missing those analyses."

The issue that Ken had identified was the very issue that had caused Ivan to start researching the product performance a few weeks ago. For reasons unknown, the product had started off hitting the projections but lately had a trend that looked like it had been dropped straight off of a cliff.

"No, not yet. My team is researching it right now. I've promised to give Tom an ETA for the research being completed later this week." Without thinking about it, Jamie also shifted into her executive mode, her own curiosity superseding the animosity that initially dogged her responses to Ken. "Based on what you've learned and reviewed so far, do you have any theories about what may be causing the problem?"

"Not really. I mean, the first thing that came to my mind is that the customers just couldn't afford the rate increases, but then I saw that the customers were dropping out while the rates were still lower than the average rates available on the market right now."

"Yeah, we were thinking that some customers may have experienced spikes in their normal monthly usage at the same time as the rates increased. That's one of the angles that Ivan is investigating."

"Hmm. Maybe. Will you let me know what you all find out?"

"Of course. That's my job. By the way, did you receive a meeting planner from Hyo? Tom has asked that my team meet with you to discuss all of the product performance trends every day until you're up to speed."

Ken had collected his report copies and was now heading back to the door. "Yeah, I got it. And I've definitely got a lot of catching up to do."

"Just so that you know, I don't expect to join most of the meetings. I'll probably just join the first one to help kick things off, but then Ivan, Julia, and Sam can take it from there."

Ken undoubtedly knew that Jamie was strategically minimizing their contact. He gave her a doleful look before opening the door. "OK, that works. See you later?"

"Not if I see you first." Jamie smiled at him before she remembered that she was peeved with him. Their discussion about the Postern performance had briefly suspended her anger, and she was able to envision the benefits of having a new ally at work. But sleeping with the ally was a bridge that she couldn't yet bring herself to cross.

"Careful now, Jamie. You might remember that you like me." Ken smiled, flashing his perfect teeth before exiting the office.

Rather than dwell on her problems with him, Jamie pulled out her copies of the reports that they had just discussed. There was a puzzle in the pages that must be solved with superhuman speed, and Jamie would not rest until she understood exactly what had caused the Postern product to blow up in all of their faces. Her instincts again screamed that Jacob already knew the reason—and that reason must place the failure at his feet. And though she didn't think that he would ever tell her the truth, she still needed to ask him what he might know as soon as she could arrange a meeting with him.

## CHAPTER 5

*While flowers may surround your feet,
your life is lived at eye level.*

BEFORE RENDEZVOUSING IN San Francisco last month, Jamie and Ken had viewed several websites that showcased the city's stunning scenery. And they had envisioned visiting as many sights as they could pack into their weekend stay. But once there, they had instead quickly fallen into their typical habit of neglecting any attractions outside of their hotel. Despite their prior resolve, they had hastened back to their room –and their bed—after eating breakfast. Now yet again, they were naked and talking like they always did after sating their passions.

"When was the last time you were in love with someone?" Ken wove his fingers with Jamie's as he gazed into her eyes. His back was resting against the headboard as Jamie sat atop him, her bare breasts inches from his lips. She could feel his warm breath on her neck as he leaned in to deliver yet another round of random kisses on her skin.

"It's been a long, long time." Jamie's skin tingled wonderfully under his leisurely care, her senses so consumed that she said nothing more until his attention ceased.

Several seconds and deep breaths later, she confessed, "Years. What about you?"

"I've never been in love."

"Never?" Jamie was surprised. She peered into his eyes.

"Nope. There were times when I thought I was in love, but then I realized that it was only lust."

"How would you figure that out?"

"Because when the sex got old, I realized that the conversation was boring. Sometimes when the women would talk to me about things that had happened in their lives, I would start feeling like I was trapped in an episode of *Charlie Brown*. And I just wanted to get out."

"That's too bad." She placed his hands on top of her shoulders, at which point he slowly ran them down, first caressing her breasts before traveling onward to rest at the small of her back as she moved closer. "But maybe you're lucky. Love is hard on the heart."

"You think so?" He shifted and began to raise them both up before slowly lowering down their bodies such that Jamie now laid on her back and he rested atop her.

"I know so." Ken kissed her, and she could feel him growing aroused.

"I guess I'll have to take your word for it." He kissed her chin and then her neck while simultaneously lowering his body to melt into hers. Jamie gasped with pleasure, lost in the language that required no words.

71

That was the way it had always been with Ken. Easy. Simple. And each of those moments was permanently etched in Jamie's memory. Only now they were accompanied by resentment and a growing feeling that she was trapped as Ken seemed to use every reason he could think of to stop by her office. He wanted to go to lunch; he wanted to discuss a potential product idea; he wanted to creep further into her space. But all Jamie wanted was to flee, to get away from the man who had single-handedly transformed her work life into some kind of hell.

And tonight, she would escape. Tonight, Jamie was meeting a former college classmate, Reed Phillips, out for dinner at a high-end restaurant named Pazmeel. She and Reed had been study partners while in college fifteen years ago, and during those years, they had formed a friendship that was akin to that of siblings. Everyone had known that Reed was Jamie's "big brother" on campus. Looking back, it was hard to believe that they had lost touch after graduating. She had once envisioned him as a permanent fixture in her life, but they had not communicated until very recently, when he sent her an e-mail on LinkedIn. According to his LinkedIn profile, Reed had been living in Baton Rouge for at least ten years, but he had not updated his profile lately, so she didn't yet know when he had moved to Houston. Tonight was as good a time as any for them to catch up for the first time in more than a decade. And even better, the plans with Reed had given her an honest excuse to decline Ken's dinner invitation earlier that day.

She arrived at Pazmeel a little earlier than planned and decided to use the time to mellow out with a glass of wine. Upon entering the restaurant, her first impression was that it was a pretty stuffy place. The dining area was large and open, but the entire mode of decor was dark, with mahogany wood-paneled walls and dreary maroon carpet, a theme that seemed to further inspire her morbid mood. She also noticed that there were very few customers, a sign that didn't bode well for the quality of the food.

Jamie gave her name to the hostess and was promptly escorted to the back of the restaurant to a table located a few paces from the kitchen. Within a few moments of being seated, she realized that, contrary to her initial apprehensions, the scents that drifted from the kitchen were quite appetizing, and her stomach began to growl. She asked the waiter to bring her a glass of their best wine and then checked her watch before reviewing the menu. She wasn't feeling adventurous enough to try any of the more exotic dishes, so she carefully eyed the options that were made with ingredients she could pronounce.

"Jamie Dubois. I can hardly believe that it's you after all of these years!"

Jamie looked up from the menu to see Reed in a chef's coat, which did little to hide the slightly swollen belly beneath it. Other than that, he looked the same—tanned, smooth skin, naturally curly hair, and a stalwart build.

Thrilled to see her long-lost friend, Jamie sprang to her feet and practically threw herself into his waiting, open arms. "Reed! It's so good to see you!" She pulled away to look up into his eyes. "You look great! Actually, you look the same as you did in college."

"Thank you, but we both know that that's a lie. I've got this tire hanging around my waistline now." He laughed and appraised Jamie now that she was standing up. "But you sure do look the same. Except that you've cut off all of your hair. Why'd you do that? You know what the Bible says about a woman's hair! It's your glory."

Jamie giggled and self-consciously touched her hair, which was cut within a breath of her scalp around the sides and the back, although a decent length was cropped on top. It was all about low maintenance. "A woman's hair is a man's glory," she laughed. "I never cared much for it."

"Well, hair or no hair, you still look good, so I'm sure that you landed some lucky man." He gestured toward the table before she could respond. "Have a seat so we can catch up!"

Jamie complied and returned to her seat as Reed sat to her left at the table. "Gosh, it's good to see you! I was so surprised to hear from you the other day."

"I've been trying to connect with several people from the college days. We had some good times back then."

"We sure did, but everyone scattered with the four winds after graduation. I haven't kept up with hardly anyone we knew in college." She indicated his chef attire. "What's with the coat? Do you work here?"

"Oh, I didn't tell you? I'm the executive chef here. Just took the job a few weeks ago."

"Really? I saw on your LinkedIn profile that you were a restaurateur, but I didn't realize that you were also a chef. That's awesome! What made you decide to become a chef?"

"Corporate America made me decide to become a chef. I did the whole rat-race thing for several years and realized that I couldn't go through life working for someone else and hoping for a fair handshake. I had to create my own opportunities. And since I've always loved to cook, I enrolled in Le Cordon Bleu and left the corporate grind behind after I earned my certificate. Eventually, I opened up my own restaurant in Baton Rouge, but it went belly-up earlier this year—along with my marriage."

The lanky male waiter who had taken Jamie's order for wine approached the table to now take the order for her entrée.

"Jamie, I want you to order whatever you want. It's on me."

"Thanks, Reed, but I can pay for—"

"I'm sure that you can afford to pay for your meal. I saw on LinkedIn that you're a big-time VP, but I'm asking you to let me, as a gentleman, treat you like a lady." He was teasing her but also unwilling to take *no* for an answer.

"All right, Reed. Thank you." Jamie normally had a hard time accepting men's generosity because she didn't want to provoke any false assumptions that she owed them something in return. But she was comfortable letting Reed preempt her monocratic ways. In keeping with her decision to select something simple, she ordered a dish named chicken roulade, which was made with ingredients that she recognized.

"Good choice." Reed turned to the waiter. "Tony, would you please bring that out, and"—he again looked at Jamie—"did you want anything to drink?"

Jamie hesitated, remembering that she had ordered wine and instantly feeling embarrassed for Tony, who appeared to have forgotten about it. "I ordered a glass of wine before you came over."

Reed turned back to the waiter, who was now blushing slightly. "Would you please bring the lady a glass of wine? Immediately?"

"Yes, chef, I'll get it right now." Tony apologized to Jamie and hurried away.

"It's service like that that is running this place into the ground." Reed scowled. "The food here is good, really good, but you can't have poor service and expect your customers to keep coming. Once word spreads that you have to ask for a drink five times before you get it, people stop coming, and they warn their friends not to come. That's why we've got a ghost town in one of the hottest districts on a Friday night."

"I was wondering about that when I walked in." They both surveyed the dining room, which now had around twenty customers and twenty-five empty tables. Jamie once again noted how awful the decor was as well. She was no expert, but the color palette was so gloomy that she would think twice about returning regardless of whether the service improved.

"I have a lot of damage control to do here. The owner is hoping that I can bring a new attitude to the place, maybe update the menu a little, hire a few new waiters and sous chefs."

"Sounds like a lot of work." Jamie could see that his heart wasn't in it. "I'm sorry to hear about your restaurant and your marriage, though. What happened, if you don't mind my asking?"

"Let's dispense with the formalities, OK? We haven't talked in a long time, but you're still my little sister, and I'm still your big brother. We're family."

Feeling as though she had just been transported back to their college days, Jamie grinned like a much younger girl. "OK."

"Good. Now that that's settled..." He exhaled a long breath. "I started up a Cajun restaurant that I had been thinking about for years, ya know? The menu, the spices I would use, the dining-room layout, all of that. It was going to be my launching pad to financial freedom—my stake in the ground, if you will." He paused, noticeably dejected by the very different outcome of his dream. "It was a risk, and the wife wasn't happy about it because I sunk all of our savings into it. She thought that I was crazy, and I thought that I would prove her wrong. The rest is history."

"You lost all of your money?"

"And then some. We're in two hundred thousand dollars of debt."

Jamie gulped air, reflexively dismayed with the debt even though it wasn't hers. "I'm sorry to hear that."

Just then, Tony discreetly set down her glass of wine and hastily scampered away before his presence could be acknowledged.

Reed seemed glad to oblige Tony's desire to be ignored. "Not as much as my wife. She put me out a couple of months ago, and I had to live with one of my buddies until I got this job. It's been tough, but I'm resilient. I'll land on my feet."

"Do you think that you and your wife will reconcile?"

He shrugged. "I dunno. Right now, we don't know if we want to. Lotta anger there between us. She's mad about the money, and I'm mad about the way she behaved while I was trying to make the restaurant work. A man needs a wife who's gonna support him and his dreams. And it just seems like she was rooting for me to fail."

"I'm sure that that's not true." As a woman, Jamie guessed that Reed's perspective about his wife's point of view was highly flawed.

"That's the truth the way I see it." Reed tapped the tabletop with all ten fingers and brightened up. "Anyway, let's talk about you. Are you married or what?" He glanced at Jamie's fingers, which were in plain sight since she was sipping her wine. "I don't see a ring. Are you single?"

"Yep, still single and still accumulating reasons to stay that way." Jamie again drank from her glass, but this time she took a large gulp. If she didn't need to drive home, she would have ordered something much stronger than wine.

"Spoken like a deeply cynical woman." He paused to scrutinize her more closely. "I don't remember you being like that in college. What's happened to you? Some guy broke your heart?"

"Not one guy. More like several guys have broken my heart since the last time we spoke. In fact, I think I had a run on every worthless man under the age of forty before I finally got ahold of myself and stopped the madness."

"Now that's hard to believe! You were always so stubborn and hard for guys to get next to in college. I remember when guys used to ask me for advice on how to get your attention because you wouldn't give them any play."

"I dated a couple of guys in college, but I kept it to a minimum because I had to keep my grades up or lose my scholarship. You know that." Jamie laughed.

"Yeah, I know, but you were practically on lockdown." Reed also laughed at the memories. "So I guess that you graduated and just went crazy."

Jamie smirked. "Yeah, I guess I did." She swallowed a larger helping of wine. "I gave a lot of myself for nothing but lies and cheating in return. Frankly, I'm embarrassed to tell you how dumb I was, but at least I can say that I've gotten smarter since then."

"Oh really? So what's different now?"

"What's different is that I decided that I'm better when I'm not in love with anyone. I keep things simple now, and I let my mind instead of my emotions rule the day."

"And how's that working out for you?" Reed's skepticism was obvious.

She slumped and drank more wine instead of answering.

"That's what I figured because you've had your bottom lip stuck out since you got here."

"I have not!" Jamie was surprised that Reed could still so ably read her body language despite not seeing her for so many years.

"Yeah, you have. You're sticking your lip out the way you did when that guy..." Reed snapped his fingers and gazed in a different direction. "What was his name? Something crazy. Oh yeah...Sebastian, a.k.a Slim Dawg." He chuckled. "You had your lip stuck out for almost six months when you found out that he had two-timed you with some other girl on campus. That's the way you look tonight. You've got your lip stuck out."

"Maybe I do." He had cornered her, but it was OK. She didn't mind coming clean with Reed. "OK, I do." Jamie had to laugh at herself.

"Denial is a bad thing, Jamie. Remember that," Reed joked. "Now tell me about the guy who got under your skin despite all of the defenses that you put up around yourself."

Jamie playfully punched his thick shoulder. "Shut up! It's not like that."

"Hey! That hurt!" Reed rubbed his arm with an exaggerated expression of pain on his face. "OK, it's not like that. Then tell me how it is. I'm listening." He folded his arms and made himself more comfortable in his chair.

"Well, I've been dating this guy named Ken for almost a year, and things were going really well. He lived in Miami; I live in Houston. It was perfect."

"Let me stop you right there," Reed interjected. "You call dating a man who lives a thousand miles away from you perfect? What kind of strange woman are you?"

"It's perfect because I work a lot of hours, and I don't have a lot of time to date."

"Uh-huh. You mean that you didn't want him to get too close to your emotions."

"Would you stop interrupting me and let me finish, please? Jeez."

"I'm sorry. Proceed."

"OK. So, like I said, he was living in Miami, but I found out on Monday that he had moved to Houston and taken a job at my company without telling me first."

Reed's first reaction was shock, and he gaped at her. Then he unexpectedly threw his head back and howled with laughter.

"What the heck is so funny?"

"Wait, wait!" Reed waved off Jamie's question. "Let me get this straight. He moved to Houston, and now he's working with you? What's his job? Does he work in a different department or what?"

"He's the VP of one of our departments."

At this additional information, Reed laughed even harder. "Now that is game! Ken is one undercover brother!"

Jamie was rapidly becoming flustered. "What do you mean?"

"I mean that he was really smooth, the way he did that, moving to Houston and putting you in a position where you have to see him every day. And now he can scope you out, you know? See how you're spending your time when he normally isn't around. Man, I wish that I could've done that before I married my wife. I didn't know what I was getting until the ring was on her finger. Then all of her true colors came out."

"So that's what you think this is all about? Some sort of game?"

"Nah, I'm not saying that. I don't know the guy. It just sounds like he's checking out his investment up close and personal before he takes your relationship to the next level. And I'm sure that he got a sweet deal with the new job as well. Most business-minded men are very motivated by money."

"And what if I don't want to take our relationship to the next level?"

Reed now regarded Jamie with a serious eye. "Do you want to?"

"No! Not right now. And not with someone I work with. Having him at the office is really awkward for me."

"Did you tell him that?"

"Not in those words, but it doesn't matter. He refuses to take a job somewhere else."

"Of course he refuses to get another job! He's got everything he wants under one roof." Reed seemed to admire Ken's audacity and cleverness. "I like this Ken guy. He has set himself up to thoroughly check you out. And I'll bet that he's watching and listening to everything that people say and do around the office where you're concerned."

"What he's done is set himself up to suffocate me. Seeing him nearly every day is already old."

"If you don't like seeing him every day, then at least you know that you definitely don't want to marry him." He laughed again. "But if you want my advice, I'd recommend that you think long and hard before you dump the guy because your mouth is saying one thing, but that stuck-out lip is saying something entirely different."

Reed's advice mirrored Layla's and only intensified Jamie's dissatisfaction with Ken, particularly since Reed seemed to think that Ken was using the situation to spy on her. She frowned as Tony appeared from nowhere and carefully placed her meal down before her.

"Thank you, Tony."

"You're welcome, ma'am. Would you like more wine?"

"Yes, thank you." While talking to Reed, Jamie had drained her glass dry.

"Uh, no, thank you," Reed pronounced. "The lady has to drive home tonight."

"I can handle another glass of wine, Reed," Jamie fussed.

"Nope, not tonight. Tony, bring her a glass of water." Reed pushed his chair back and stood up as Tony rushed away. "Go ahead and eat before your food gets cold. I don't want you leaving here with an empty stomach since you put away that wine like some kind of slovenly alcoholic." Reed had always relentlessly teased Jamie, and they both snickered good-naturedly at the dig.

"All right, sir, I'll try to clean my plate." It wouldn't be hard to do since fancy restaurants like Pazmeel offered very little food in return for their sky-high prices. Her plate contained a few morsels of chicken, a dab of creamy mashed potatoes, and three small stalks of grilled asparagus.

"And let me know what you think about it. I'll be back in around twenty minutes to check on you."

"OK, thanks." She picked up the dinner fork as he walked away, but her thoughts had already been whisked eons from this place. Reed's perspective about Ken's motives for joining Radian had never crossed her mind, and she wondered whether they had any merit. Spying on his supposed investment? On the surface, it sounded pretty shady.

Jamie looked around the restaurant as she chewed a bit of the chicken, which was actually quite tasty. Reed had been right. The food was definitely good. Unfortunately, he was also right that the restaurant was in big trouble. While they had been talking, three of the previously occupied tables had been cleared, which left around six tables with customers. No new customers had arrived, and a couple of waiters were standing near the door, loitering with the hostess. If things didn't improve soon, Reed would be out of another job.

As another set of customers rose to leave, Jamie thought about how lonely the restaurant was. A battery of additional descriptions also came unbidden to her mind: dull, dreary, drab, bland—even better, depressed. Or maybe she was describing herself.

# CHAPTER 6

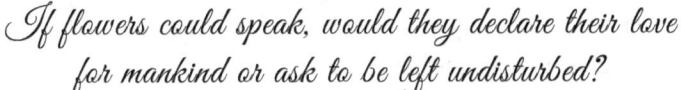

*If flowers could speak, would they declare their love for mankind or ask to be left undisturbed?*

"EVERY MORNING, I wake up and say to myself, 'You can do this. You can live well. You'll be all right without Paul,'" Layla glumly remarked as she and Jamie meandered through the aisles at a Whole Foods grocery store on Saturday afternoon. "It's still hard to believe that it's come to this. When we said 'for better or for worse' on our wedding day, I never imagined that the *worse* could be so bad."

"No one ever does." Jamie inspected the ingredients on the label of a marinade while she spoke. "But you never know what may happen. Paul might get his act together now that you've put some heat under him."

"Girl, we don't need that marinade. I make everything from scratch, and my sauces are way better than anything you can buy at any grocery store."

"OK, fine with me." Jamie set the jar back down and continued to roll their basket down the aisle. As a woman with no cooking skills, she was perfectly fine with accepting Layla's guidance on all things food. So far, they had loaded their basket with a variety of fresh vegetables, fruits, spices, poultry, and tilapia, passing by the packages of beef and pork with hardly a glance since Layla preferred not to feed either type of meat to Sadie and Luke, both of whom were spending the day with Paul and his parents.

"He's a stubborn man. And he's used to getting his way."

"Does that surprise you? You've treated him like a king since high school."

They had reached the aisle with soups, rice, and pasta. Layla began to place more items in the basket based on the dishes that she had decided to prepare over the next week. At Jamie's assurance before they had come to the store, Layla selected whatever items she wanted. Jamie insisted on paying for everything since Layla and the kids were guests at her house.

"This pasta costs too much." Layla balked at a seventeen-ounce box of whole wheat spaghetti. "Why do people pay seven dollars for this little bit of pasta? That's crazy."

"It's expensive because it's organic. Just put it in the basket if that's what you want. I don't care about the price."

"All right, but we could get a better deal at Walmart." Layla dropped the pasta into the basket with a crestfallen expression on her face. "I treated him like a king because I wanted him to know that he was important."

"Mission accomplished. But unfortunately, he thinks that he's more important than everyone else, including his own kids."

"I know. His head is bigger than a blimp, and I probably did create the monster. I just didn't want to treat him the way Mama treated Daddy. I've always thought that Daddy might've stuck around if she had shown him more love." Their parents had divorced before Jamie was twelve. And both Mama and Daddy had seemed immensely glad to be rid of each other.

"She couldn't give him something that she didn't have. The only reason they got married was because she got pregnant."

"But I missed having Daddy at the house when they split up."

"I did, too, at first. But he stayed involved with our lives. He didn't divorce us." Now they had reached the paper products. "We need to get a barrel of these paper towels because the kids have already gone through the napkins that I had."

"OK." They both tossed several rolls of paper towels into the basket, after which Jamie also reached for jumbo packages of toilet paper. "And we need to get some better cleaners, too. I noticed some smudges of ketchup on my coffee table the other day."

"Jamie, I'm sorry. I'll do a better job of keeping the kids in the dining room when they're eating. They know better than that."

"Don't worry about it. I do want them to eat in the dining room, but I'm not dumb enough to think that they won't sneak out from time to time. Remember how mad Mama used to get at us for leaving bread and cake crumbs all over the couch when we were growing up?" They both remembered all too well and laughed.

"Mama seemed like she was always mad about something. She wasn't like that until she divorced Daddy."

Jamie perused the glass cleaners and selected a couple to drop into the basket. "Yeah, being a single parent is a lot of work. And she didn't want us to make the same mistakes that she made."

"But I did, didn't I?" Layla suddenly stopped short. "I made the same mistakes. And I brought two children into a bad situation like she did."

Jamie turned to peer directly into Layla's eyes. "Don't think like that. You and Paul are not Mama and Daddy. You got married because you loved each other. It's just that somewhere along the line, despite everything you tried to be to him, the train came off the tracks. That has nothing to do with our parents."

"I tried, Jamie. I tried so hard to do everything that a good wife is supposed to do for her husband."

"But you can't make a grown man be something or someone he doesn't want to be. That's not your fault or your burden."

Layla closed her eyes and nodded. "You're right. I did the best that I could." They began to move down the aisle again, eventually turning a corner to scan the vast array of body washes and lotions.

"I really do hate that you've been going through such a tough time, Layla. I don't think that anyone in the family has understood how much you've been hurting and struggling." Jamie dropped soap into the basket as she spoke.

They then began to wheel the cart toward the checkout area. The lines for all of the cashiers were a mile long.

"I know. I was just thinking about holding things together with Paul and ignoring the truth that we should never have been together in the first place. But I won't be doing that anymore. I'm going to put myself first from now on."

"Good. Nothing wrong with that."

"There's also nothing wrong with you taking it a little easy on Ken."

Jamie huffed as they inched forward in the checkout line. "I wish that you'd let that go."

"If you don't want him, why haven't you thrown those roses away?"

"That would be dumb. They're not dead yet."

"Uh-huh. I think you haven't thrown them out because you like him more than you want to admit. And you like those roses, too."

Jamie smacked and twisted her lips. "Whatever."

"He's not Dwight. Just like I'm not Mama."

"I know that." Jamie's defenses were now thrown up.

"He's not Ellis, Jonathan, or Teddy either." While Ellis had taught Jamie the pitfalls of dating a coworker, the latter two men had deepened her disgust for liars and cheaters. After dating for a year, Jonathan had ditched her for his ex-wife, while Teddy had eventually admitted to being gay.

Jamie pretended to ignore Layla's comments.

"You used to glow when you talked about Ken. Did you know that?"

"Glow how?"

"You used to light up whenever you described one of your trips with him. Like when you got back from New Orleans a few months ago. You were so happy that you lit up the room."

"Maybe I did. But those days are over."

Layla merely tsk-tsked at Jamie's stubbornness.

When the sisters finally made it out of the grocery store, they went straight back to Jamie's house and began to carry in the multitude of grocery bags that were stacked on top of each other in Jamie's car. Not long after she set down the first round of bags on one of the granite kitchen counters, Jamie realized that her cell phone was ringing and dug through her cluttered purse to find it. Before answering the call, she looked at the caller ID, saw that it was Ken, and contemplated letting the call roll into voice mail. But if she avoided his calls, he might corner her at work like he had done throughout the week. Once again feeling trapped, she answered the call with a bad attitude.

"Hello?"

"Hey, Jamie. Where have you been? I've been trying to reach you for a few hours."

"I was at the grocery store with Layla. What's up?" Her annoyance was immediately aggravated by his expectation that she should tell him why he couldn't reach her sooner.

"Oh, OK. I thought that you were avoiding me." He gave a lame chuckle as Jamie remained silent. She heard him clear his throat uncomfortably. "So did you have a good time with your friend last night?"

"Yeah, it was nice." Layla was still carrying grocery bags into the kitchen, so Jamie moved out of her way since she was blocking Layla's route.

"That's good." He paused as though waiting for Jamie to say something more, but she again remained silent, her irritation heightening with each passing second. "I was wondering if you'd like to get together tonight. Maybe catch a movie or get some dinner?"

"No can do, Ken. I'm staying in tonight. I brought some work home that I need to catch up on before Monday."

"So you're not planning to do anything this weekend?"

"I'm planning to spend my weekend the way that I always spend it—reading reports. You know that's what I normally do."

"I know, but I thought that you could take a break from that tonight. I haven't seen much of the city yet, and you haven't seen my apartment downtown. We could make a night of it."

"Sorry, Ken, but I can't tonight." Once again, Layla was bringing in another bag of groceries and passed by just in time to hear this response. She threw Jamie a curious look before heading back to the garage for more bags. "I'm behind with a lot of work because of the extra meetings that I attended to start bringing you up to speed on everything." She couldn't hide the animosity in her voice.

Now it was Ken's turn to be silent and Jamie's turn to wait. She assumed that he was trying to choose his next words carefully. "Jamie, can we get past this?"

"I don't know."

"OK, let me ask the question a different way: do you want to get past this?"

"I don't know."

More silence. Jamie felt Bear's paws on her legs and picked him up.

"You're pushing me away."

Again electing to withhold a response, Jamie waited to hear him disconnect. To her chagrin, he didn't.

"Hello? Are you there?"

"I'm here, Ken."

"I'm not going to stick around and be treated like this. If you want me to stop calling you, tell me now."

"I don't know what I want. The truth is that I've never thought beyond weekend trips with you. And now that you've moved to Houston, I'm not going to drop everything just because you have nothing to do."

Layla had walked back into the kitchen with the last set of grocery bags and had begun to unpack them. When she heard Jamie's last statement, she halted all movement and began to openly stare at Jamie with an astonished look.

"OK, I have my answer. Have a good weekend." Ken finally hung up, releasing Jamie from the unwanted call, but not from her ire. She put her cell phone down and looked at Layla.

"If Ken is half a man, he won't be calling you anymore."

"I don't care." Jamie put Bear down and walked over to the stuffed grocery bags. Layla quizzically and wordlessly eyed her before joining her in unpacking them.

# CHAPTER 7

— ❧ —

*Love does not yield
a field of flowers.*

DID SHE CARE? Although Jamie had played it cool with Layla, the truth was that Ken had said something that struck a long-dormant chord of emotion that was making Jamie somewhat uncomfortable. He had used the phrase "pushing me away," which implied he thought that they were close. It suggested intimacy beyond the limits she had placed on their relationship, the exact sort of intimacy that Jamie had been running from for three years. She admitted nothing to Layla, but a myriad of insecurities were beginning to shred the tacit ropes that bound them inside. And she couldn't stop thinking about the roses. Those damned roses, which she had recently placed in her last unused guest room to avoid looking at them. But even though she couldn't see them, she knew that they were there. And this knowing seemed to keep bringing Ken to mind along with his accusation that she was pushing him away.

She wasn't ready to deal with any of this—not the questions, the emotions, or the confusion that was slowly overtaking her. And until she was ready, Jamie decided that she had to get the roses out of her house. She had to

be free of whatever beguiling influence they were plant-
ing in her thoughts. So while Layla began preparations for
that evening's dinner, Jamie quickly grabbed a jacket and
headed next door to see her neighbor, Charlotte, with the
vase of withering roses.

A widow in her midfifties, Charlotte had lost her husband of thirty years to pancreatic cancer long before Jamie
had moved into the neighborhood. He had passed away
within a mere five months of being diagnosed, a crushing
loss that had paradoxically left her with a profound faith in
the eternal nature and beauty of love. Charlotte's personal
story and perspectives couldn't have been more different
from Jamie's. She believed that she had known more love
in her years than most people experienced in their entire
lifetimes. And despite her husband having died much too
soon, she was irrevocably grateful to have had the gift of
his love.

In keeping with her deep appreciation for the beauty
of love, Charlotte also found great joy in beautiful things
that reminded her of love, a virtue that had motivated her
to both open a small flower shop and to maintain a miniature greenhouse in her backyard. Although Charlotte
and Jamie didn't share the same view on flowers, the two
had nevertheless formed a very warm friendship. And
over the years, they had discovered that they did have a
few things in common, among them an appreciation for a
picturesque sunset, sometimes punctuated with a glass of
Pinot Noir after a long day. They also discovered that an
ever-so-gentle Charlotte could not coax Jamie to amend

her petulant point of view about the flowers that Charlotte loved so well.

Upon reaching Charlotte's porch, Jamie rang the doorbell and shivered impatiently in the cold. It was a chilly forty-five degrees, which merited an insulated coat, but Jamie had opted for a light jacket, having mistakenly assumed that she would be outside for only a couple of minutes. After one long minute with no answer, she rang the doorbell again, certain that Charlotte was at home because she had seen her come outside to check her mail a short time ago.

Guessing that Charlotte might be tending to her prized cache of flowers in the greenhouse, Jamie decided to venture to the backyard, entering it through a gate that Charlotte habitually neglected to lock. The greenhouse was located directly beside the garage so that it wouldn't infringe on the rest of the area reserved for Charlotte's grandchildren to play whenever they visited.

"Charlotte!" Jamie called as she walked toward the greenhouse. "Charlotte! It's Jamie." She wanted to ensure that she didn't startle Charlotte when she entered the greenhouse.

"Jamie?" she heard Charlotte respond from inside the greenhouse before opening the door and peeking out to see Jamie approaching with the drooping roses. "Hello there! Come on in!" Jamie finally reached the greenhouse and quickly strode inside the miniature glass structure as Charlotte closed the door. "It's cold out there, isn't it?"

Jamie hugged her friend as best she could with the roses in one of her hands. "Yes, too cold for me."

Charlotte released her and smiled fondly, radiating her infinitely caring nature at Jamie, who reflexively sparkled in return. There was something about Charlotte that inevitably soothed whoever she directed her attention to, and Jamie felt drawn to that calm much the way a musician was drawn to a transcendent musical note. Charlotte was a classy, well-kept lady whose slim build and vibrant green eyes belied her age. Were it not for the stray streaks of gray hair that mingled with her auburn locks, Charlotte could easily pass for someone in her early forties. She eyeballed the roses that Jamie had brought with her.

"Whatcha got there?"

"Two dozen roses that Ken gave me on Monday."

"Looks like two dozen dying roses to me."

"Well, I don't have a green thumb like you do."

"Is that why you brought them with you? You think that I want them?" Charlotte removed her gardening gloves and touched the petals, which had turned a purplish shade since Jamie had initially received them. "I already know that you don't want them." She winked at Jamie and smiled again.

"Yeah, well…" Jamie looked at the flowers. "I don't know. Maybe I do, maybe I don't."

"It sure doesn't look like you want them. You could've given 'em a little vinegar and sugar if you wanted to keep them alive longer."

"Oh. I didn't know that," Jamie feebly offered.

"You could've asked me on Monday if you wanted to know."

"I've been busy. You know me."

"Yep, I know you. And I know that Ken shouldn't have given you any flowers." Charlotte chuckled and again looked at the blooms. "I'll bet that they were really something to see on Monday."

Jamie was characteristically apathetic. "I guess they were. A lot has changed since Monday."

"Are we still talking about the roses? I noticed that your sister's car has been at your house every day this week. What's going on?"

Jamie spotted an empty space on one of the shelves and set down the roses. "She's going through a rough patch right now, so I'm letting her and the kids stay with me for a while."

"That's very nice of you. And I'm sure that she appreciates it. But you seem a little tense. Is something bothering you?" Charlotte softly touched Jamie's back, again exuding the comforting warmth.

"Oh, I just don't know what to do with the roses."

"Honey, those roses are almost dead. There's nothing that you can do with them at this point."

"I understand. I—" Confounded, she looked away from Charlotte toward a pot of blooming gardenias, which she knew to have a distinctly perfumed fragrance. Jamie deeply inhaled the mixture of sweet scents that permeated the modest structure, allowing herself to appreciate the symphony of fragrances if not their origins. "Your greenhouse smells like a slice of heaven."

"I know. That's one of the reasons that I like to come in here." Charlotte moved toward a prodigious flower that was mixed with creamy white and rich magenta shades. "You see this lily? It reminds me of Walter. It was the first flower that he brought to me on our very first date. Such a lovely, lovely flower." She dipped her nose into the bloom and inhaled the fragrance before moving on to a different, violet flower. "And this one, this daisy. It's so proud. See the way it shows off its long, gorgeous petals? It's asking the world to look at it and to love it in all of its quiet glory." She ran her fingertips along the petals, momentarily absorbed with her appreciation for the daisy as Jamie silently watched. "This daisy reminds me of you."

"Really?" Jamie was genuinely surprised. "Why?"

"Because you have so much pride, and yet underneath it all, you really just want to be loved like everyone else."

"I've got plenty of love," Jamie protested.

"I suspect that you do," Charlotte agreed. "You just don't know what to do with it, which is why you brought those roses over here."

"I wasn't talking about that sort of love."

"But I am." Charlotte maneuvered herself around Jamie in the small space and crossed back to the dying roses. "You've often said that flowers are meaningless when a man gives them to a woman. And there is some truth to that, depending on the man. But it's not true of all men, especially when they love the woman they've given the flowers to." She looked from the roses to Jamie. "If he loves you, then the flowers symbolize his love because their beauty reminded him of the woman he felt compelled to give them to."

"Ken didn't buy the flowers because he loves me," Jamie promptly corrected her friend. "He bought them because he felt guilty about doing something stupid."

"Fine, so let's pretend that we're not talking about Ken or these roses per se." Charlotte walked away from the roses and closer to Jamie. "We're just talking about flowers and love."

Jamie sighed listlessly. "You already know my opinion about all of that."

"Indeed I do, but humor me."

"All right," Jamie resignedly sighed again.

"When a man genuinely loves a woman, he begins to see the world with his soul every time he thinks about her. He doesn't realize it, of course, but that's what happens to him. And suddenly, the roses and orchids and lilies, things that he never paid attention to before, are alive and brilliant because they remind him of the woman he loves. It's as though his love for a woman has brought him closer to God and awakened him to all of the natural splendor around him for the first time in his life. That's why women attach so much meaning to the flowers we receive from men we love."

"I understand, but we can't assume that the flowers mean that the men love us."

"I'm not denying that. If he loves you, you'll know it even if he never brings you a single flower. You'll feel it when he looks at you or touches you because his soul is reaching out to yours in a way that simply cannot be explained." Charlotte lightly rubbed Jamie's arm. "Just trust me. You'll know." She turned back to the roses. "But as for these roses, you'll never know what to do with them unless you're in love and you know that they were given to you because you are loved in return. And while you try to figure it all out, you'll have to take them back home with you."

"There's nothing to figure out. Can't I just leave them here on this shelf for a few days?"

"Nope. They don't belong here." She winked and smiled. "The good news is that they won't be troubling you for much longer."

Jamie's visit with Charlotte had not gone as planned, and she grudgingly tramped back home with the roses and even greater distress than when she had arrived at Charlotte's house. She knew that Charlotte meant well, but all of her talk about flowers and love had left Jamie with more weariness, more dissatisfaction, and more of the restlessness that had driven her to Charlotte's house in the first place.

Disheartened, Jamie opened her front door and was immediately beset by the mouthwatering aroma of onions and spices that she couldn't identify. Following her nose, she headed straight for the kitchen, where Layla was busily adding salt and fresh thyme to something frying in a skillet.

"It smells fantastic in here! What are you making?"

"It's my version of fried potatoes, not to be mistaken for French fries. The kids love it, so I'm making it for dinner." Layla briefly diverted her eyes to Jamie while stirring the contents in the skillet. "Why are you walking around with those roses?"

"Ugh, don't ask." Jamie hastily went to the utility room and placed the roses on top of the washing machine, which was perhaps their tenth roost in the house since Monday, and went back to the kitchen. She noticed that, in addition to the skillet full of potatoes, there was another pot simmering with more goodies. She pulled the top off to see baby carrots as a tangy fragrance wafted from the pot. "Do you mind if I taste one of these?"

"Of course not. Help yourself." Layla handed Jamie a small fork from a nearby drawer filled with silverware and then went back to stirring the frying potatoes.

Jamie used the fork to select one of the carrots, placed the lid back on the pot, and then commenced to blowing on the steaming prize to help it cool faster. When she finally tasted it, she was pleasantly delighted with the assortment of sweet flavors that overwhelmed her palate.

"Ooh, this is delicious! What did you put on the carrots?"

"Just some honey, a little orange juice, a pinch of apricot." She looked at Layla and smiled. "You like 'em, huh?"

"I don't just like them. I love them! I could eat the whole pot by myself!"

"Yeah, they are pretty good." Layla turned off the burner under the potatoes. "And I'd like to see you eat something for dinner besides those frozen Stouffer's dinners in your freezer. I've never seen anyone eat so much processed food."

"If I could cook like you, I would never eat another frozen dinner again." Jamie giggled and then fell silent for a few moments, ruminating on an idea that had occurred to her. "You know, a friend of mine just moved to Houston and is the executive chef at a ritzy restaurant downtown named Pazmeel. Ever heard of it?"

"No, why?" Layla had pulled out a broiling pan, laid some tilapia filets in neat rows inside of it, and started seasoning the fish with cilantro and ground cumin.

"He's planning to hire some sous chefs, and if you're interested, I can ask him to consider you for one of the jobs."

"Oh my God!" Layla abruptly shrieked, setting down the seasoning on the counter beside the broiling pan. "Oh my God!" she repeated excitedly. "You would do that for me?"

"Sure, if you want me to."

Layla screamed with elation and began to happily jump up and down, grabbing Jamie and hugging her tightly. "Yes! Yes, I want you to!"

Jamie endeavored to hug her gleeful sister as she continued to jump in her arms. "OK, I'll ask him next week. I'm not promising anything. I can't make him hire you. I'm just going to ask him to give you a chance."

"Thank you!" Layla bounced around the kitchen like a child who had just been promised a trip to Disneyland, but then she halted with a questioning expression on her face. "What do sous chefs earn in a year?"

By now, Jamie was laughing at Layla's exuberant reaction. "I have no idea, but it's gotta be more than what you're making at Walmart."

"That's true." Layla considered this likelihood for a few moments and then resumed her dancing and leaping around the kitchen. "Even if it doesn't pay more, if I get the job, I'll be able to start building a real career at something I like to do!"

"Well, let's see if you get the job first, OK?" Jamie was still laughing at her sister's jubilance.

Layla ignored Jamie's caution and returned to seasoning the fish while humming a gospel song named "No Weapon." But the cheerful mood was cut short when someone rang the doorbell. Both sisters knew that it could only be Paul bringing the children back along with yet another round of drama.

Choosing not to greet Paul, Jamie went into the living room as Layla walked toward the front door, where Paul waited with Sadie and Luke. When she opened the door, Paul apparently attempted to enter the house with the kids, but Jamie heard Layla tell him that he couldn't come in.

"Why not? I thought that we could sit down like a family and have dinner together."

Layla waved the children indoors through an opening that was large enough to accommodate only their petite bodies. Seconds later, both Sadie and Luke rushed into the living room to greet Jamie, who affectionately kissed and hugged them before helping them to remove their jackets and knit winter hats. Meanwhile, Layla was stuck at the front door, trying to get Paul to leave.

"Maybe some other time, Paul, but not today. Go home."

"Layla, why are you being like this? I shouldn't have to leave you and the kids here. We should all be going home together. You're my wife. You belong with me."

"Did you get a job yet?"

"I told you already—I'm working on it."

"OK, well, until you actually start working and bringing home a paycheck, let's pretend that I'm not your wife."

"Wha—? What's gotten into you lately? I don't understand, baby. Don't you love me anymore?"

"I honestly don't know the answer to that question. But I'll tell you what I do love. I love electricity, food, gas for my car. Things that require money. Do I need to remind you that love doesn't pay the bills?"

"Aunt Jamie," Luke whined, drowning out Jamie's ability to hear Layla's and Paul's exchange, "I'm hungry."

"OK, sweetie. Your mama has almost finished cooking dinner. We'll all eat in a few minutes, OK?"

"OK. Can I have some orange juice, please?"

"Ooh! I want some juice, too, Aunt Jamie!" Sadie joined in.

"All right, let's go to the kitchen. I'll give you both some juice, but you have to promise to stay in the kitchen until you drink all of it."

"OK!" Both kids excitedly agreed in unison.

All three of them went into the kitchen, where Jamie poured them both small glasses of orange juice. Just as the kids began to drink the juice, Layla haughtily strutted back into the kitchen to finish preparing the fish before popping it in the oven.

"Is Paul gone?" Jamie put the container of orange juice back in the refrigerator.

"Of course, but I had to give him five dollars to leave." She added a tablespoon of water to the broiling pan, rapidly falling back into the mechanics of cooking.

"What? Why?"

"He said that he didn't have any money or enough gas to get home."

"Gosh." Jamie was incensed at Paul's gall. Miraculously, though, Layla seemed to have dismissed him after returning her attention to the fish.

"It's fine, Jamie. Let it go. I made sure he understands that he shouldn't come here again if he can't afford to get home on his own dime. Next time, he'll have to walk."

"Mama, we're hungry!" Sadie tugged at the tail end of Layla's magenta cotton tunic.

"OK, baby, dinner will be ready in five minutes." Layla leaned down and hugged her daughter tightly. "Mama sure did miss you while you were gone today. Did you have a good time with Daddy, Grandma, and Grandpa?"

Sadie nodded her head as Layla planted a kiss on her forehead. "We went to the movies, and then we played Color Code."

"Color Code? What's that?"

"It's a game that makes you stack a bunch of plastic thingies on top of each other," Luke explained as a six-year-old does.

"Hey, peanut! Where's my hug and kiss?" Layla playfully scolded Luke, at which point he ran into her arms beside Sadie. "I'm glad that you both had fun today. And I'm even happier that you're back."

Layla heaped her motherly love onto her children as Jamie watched. She didn't know if she wanted children, a far cry from how she had felt in her twenties when she had dated a guy named Julius. Julius the Jewel, she had called him back then. He had seemed to be so perfect, always holding the door for her, helping her with her chair like a rare gentleman. She had pictured having his babies someday—until she found out that he already had seven children with seven different women. He had waited until he thought she was too much in love to dump him before telling her. But his ploy had not worked. Soon after Jamie had learned about his small tribe of children, Julius the Jewel had become Julius the Jilted. Every now and then since, she tried to imagine herself as someone's mother, but the image was fast fading to nothing.

"You two go get washed up for dinner," Layla instructed Sadie and Luke, patting them both on their shoulders and sending them off to one of the bathrooms to wash their hands. "They sure are cute, aren't they?" Layla smiled lovingly as they disappeared into a hallway.

"Yeah, and they're good kids," Jamie agreed.

"They're the two best things that I've done in the past ten years."

Jamie nodded absentmindedly before glancing at Layla. "Well, I think that I'll go change out of these jeans so that my clothes can expand with my stomach at dinnertime."

Layla laughed and turned to the oven to peek at the fish. "All right. Dinner will be served in a few, so don't be too long."

Jamie loped toward her bedroom with Bear hot on her heels and a vague sense of emptiness that wouldn't go away.

# CHAPTER 8

*A flower's beauty never disappoints; therefore, a flower cannot be compared to love.*

As her personal life seemed to be growing strangely murky, Jamie turned more to her "Old Faithful"—her job—for some measure of comfort. The parts had always worked perfectly and logically. Normally. But not lately. And so Old Faithful had begun to let her down, particularly in this morning's roundtable with Tom, who was displaying his capacity for stern leadership. Jamie had come prepared to gloss over the Postern product issues in favor of highlighting her team's accomplishments over the past week, but he was having none of it.

"Is Ivan any closer to pinpointing the Postern issue yet, Jamie?"

"He's ruled out a few things, which certainly narrows down the list of potential causes."

"That's a rather evasive response, don't you think?"

The air was distinctly thick with awkward restlessness as her colleagues observed the exchange in silence. Jamie unthinkingly cast a quick glance at Ken, who maintained a stoic posture, before responding to Tom.

"We're committed to getting to the bottom of it by next Friday. I think we're almost there."

"What makes you so certain? Do you have information that you can share with the rest of us?"

"Well—" Now she met Jacob's eyes and thought she saw glee dancing in his. "No. I just have confidence in our plan of attack and in my team."

Tom pursed his lips. "Next Friday can't get here soon enough. I'm looking forward to hearing your findings."

Jamie nodded smartly while thinking that she hoped to actually have findings to report.

After everyone had completed their updates, they all filed out of the conference room with less buoyancy than usual. Or perhaps it was only Jamie who was lacking bounce since Tom had been so obviously displeased with her update. And there was also Ken's unusual coldness throughout the meeting. He had hardly looked at her, and something about it felt wrong. But not as wrong as Tom's apparent lack of confidence in her. That was also highly unusual. And his vexation seemed to be escalating, foreshadowing an ominous end for whatever or whoever was behind the Postern catastrophe. She remained certain that her team was in the clear, but waiting for the proof to be found was getting to be nerve-racking.

Rather than head back to her office, Jamie decided to take a detour and get a cup of coffee in the break room. Unbeknownst to her, Randall had decided to tag along.

"Hey, Jamie." He sounded breathless after almost jogging down the hallway to catch up with her. "Don't worry about Tom. I'll talk to him for you. He was pretty brutal in there."

"No need for that, Randall. Tom just wants answers, and I'll make sure he gets them." Jamie began to strategize how to get rid of Randall. She had no intention of being stuck with him in the break room and then probably all the way back to her office. The bathroom seemed like the best option, so she hung a left down a hallway that terminated in bathrooms as Randall continued to talk and walk with her.

"Of course he needs answers, but he doesn't need to grill you that way. I didn't like that at all."

"It's all right. I'm a big girl."

"You sure are." His tone had suddenly changed, his voice becoming sultrier. "You know, Jamie, I'm dying to take you out. We can go anywhere you want to go. I promise that you'll have a good time."

"No, thank you, Randall. I've already told you several times that I don't date men at work." She picked up her pace. The bathroom was maybe ten yards away.

"Can't you make an exception this one time?" Randall was beginning to pant from the exertion of keeping up with her. He was in no shape to speed walk alongside Jamie. "You may not believe it, but I'm a really fun guy. You wouldn't regret it."

"I'm sure that you are fun, but no." She had finally reached the bathroom and pushed the door open to go in. Apparently not realizing where they were, Randall remained in lockstep until Jamie stopped him. "Randall, this is the ladies' room. You can't come in here."

He glanced at the sign on the door and turned bright red. "Oh, sorry about that." He backed away, still out of breath. "I'll wait here for you."

"Don't wait for me, Randall. I might be a while." Jamie was attempting to be delicate but would spell it out, if necessary, to get free of him.

"Oh." His blush deepened to a darker shade of red. "Yes, I understand. OK, I'll leave you to your—uh—your business then."

"Thank you." She walked into the bathroom and leaned against the closed door, grateful that he was gone.

"Jamie, why are you standing against that nasty door? Don't you know how many germs are probably crawling around on it?" It was Katrina, the living office-gossip column and yet another person Jamie would prefer not to be bothered with. She was washing her hands as she cautioned Jamie.

"Hi, Katrina." Jamie walked to a sink beside the one Katrina was using and turned on the faucet to wash her own hands. "I didn't see you there. How are you?" She squirted soap onto her hands and began washing them.

"I'm good. How 'bout you? Did you find out that I was right about Jacob coming after you?" Katrina was now drying her hands as Jamie rinsed hers.

Jamie pretended disinterest, unwilling to contribute to the gossip ring. "No, I think you've been misinformed." She reached for a paper towel to dry her hands.

"That's impossible. I got my information from a prime source. Take it from me—you need to watch your back."

Jamie headed for the door.

"Are you going back to your office?" Katrina was right behind her.

"Not yet. I'm going to get some coffee."

"That sounds good. I think that I'll get some, too."

"Great." Jamie tried not to groan, displeased that she had not been able to ditch another pesky tagalong.

"Did you hear about Chantal?" Chantal was one of the staff accountants at Radian. Jamie didn't know her age, but she looked to be in her early twenties.

"Hear what?"

"She didn't get married last month."

"Yeah, I heard about that." Jamie kept moving, determined to burn rubber to the break room and then lose Katrina.

"Did you hear why?"

"No, and I don't need to."

"She made a pass at her fiancé's best friend. Didn't know the guy was gay." Katrina giggled as Jamie shuddered with her own memories of such an unexpected revelation. "Can you believe that?" Katrina had an unnerving knack for hearing about the most personal, embarrassing moments in everyone's lives.

Thankfully, they had reached the break room. Jamie kept moving swiftly to the coffee bar. "I'm really sorry to hear it. Maybe I'll go talk to her later on, make sure she's OK."

"Don't trouble yourself. I can assure you that she's OK. In fact, she's already got her eyes on a new prospect."

"Oh, well, good for her. I hope that it works out." Jamie poured a cup of coffee, focused on completing the task at hand as quickly as possible.

"If it does work out, it'll be an entertaining office soap opera for us all to watch. She's decided to go after the new guy, Kenneth, who I swear has got to be one of the finest men I've ever seen!"

Jamie flinched at the mention of Ken's name, but she remained silent while continuing the next steps of adding cream and sugar to her coffee. Katrina followed suit, still talking without interruption.

"The first time I saw him, I thought that the heavens had opened up. The man is perfection, don't you think?"

Jamie tasted her coffee, once again not responding. She knew that Katrina loved to dish the goods and could talk enough for ten people, so there was no pressure on Jamie to fill any lulls in Katrina's one-way conversation.

"Anyway, I don't blame Chantal for going after him. I heard that he's single, so he's fair game. And you know that she's going to pull out all of the stops." Now Katrina was laughing. "You should hear some of the stuff that she's talking about doing to him. It's hilarious! I can hardly wait for the show to start."

Finding her coffee tolerable, Jamie began walking to the exit without acknowledging any of Katrina's comments about Ken and Chantal. But she had heard them loud and clear. And she was definitely pissed off. The idea of Ken sleeping with Chantal was absolutely infuriating. She didn't want to believe that it was even possible for them to hook up, but the images of them together were already messing with her mind.

Once back in her office, she closed the door and coached herself to think rationally. Ken wasn't going to have sex with Chantal. She didn't need to worry about that. Was she worried about it? Why was her heart threatening to explode? What the hell was wrong with her?

She crossed the room to her desk and took a seat. The reports scattered around her desktop provided ample proof that she had more to do than time to do it. And yet here she was getting caught up in Katrina's gossip about something that had not even happened. Meanwhile, Tom was behaving as if she was letting him down, an indisputable problem that required her attention. She needed to focus on restoring Tom's faith in her—and saving her job.

This train of thought calmed her, and her breath slowed. She wouldn't keep waiting for Ivan to find the smoking gun that she needed. She would dig in and find the problem herself. She would take control of the situation and her destiny.

Acting on her newfound resolve, she spent the next few hours reviewing the Postern forecast and getting nowhere fast when someone knocked on her door. "Come in," she distractedly called out.

"This just arrived for you." Hyo, her assistant, brought in a neat package and set it down on Jamie's desk. She absolutely adored Hyo, whose family had emigrated from Korea before he had even learned to walk. He was twenty-seven years old, a whiz at everything, and Jamie's invaluable right hand.

"What's that?" Jamie was puzzled as she reached for the package and started to open it.

"I assumed that it was your lunch. You didn't order it?"

"No, I was going to ask you the same thing." Jamie pulled a plastic container from the package and saw that a note had been taped to the top that read, "Give this a taste and then give me a call." She immediately guessed that Reed was the benefactor. Jamie looked at the tiny clock on her computer screen and realized that the time was well past noon. "I didn't even realize that it was lunchtime." She also didn't understand why Reed would be sending a meal to her.

"Whatever is in there sure does smell good." Hyo curiously looked at the container that Jamie had set between them.

"It sure does." Jamie lifted a clear plastic top from the container, releasing spirals of steam and yet more pungent aromas into the air around them.

"What is that? Steak?"

"Uh-huh, steak with a side of mushrooms and—" Jamie dubiously looked more closely at one of the sides. "What's that?"

Hyo also scrutinized the dish. "I recognize the squash, but there's some other stuff mixed in that I don't think I've ever seen before."

"Hmm…" Jamie twisted her lips indecisively as Hyo peered into the original package and produced a set of plastic utensils.

"Try it and let me know how it tastes."

Jamie removed the utensils from the plastic sheath, took the fork, and offered the spoon to Hyo. "You try it, too." She and Hyo had shed all appearances of a formal relationship within months of Jamie hiring him.

"Cool!"

They both scooped up and tasted small amounts of the side dishes.

"That's delicious!" Hyo covered his mouth since he was still chewing the food. "I need the recipe for my girl-friend. If she can cook that, I might marry her."

"Cook it yourself." Jamie laughed. "This isn't 1950."

"I've heard that those were the good ole days."

"Are you trying to provoke me?"

"Who me? No way! Just crackin' jokes."

"Uh-huh. OK, let's try the steak." Jamie used a plastic knife to slice a few bite-size pieces of the steak. She and Hyo then used their respective fork and spoon to taste the heavenly smelling morsels.

"This steak just melts in your mouth," Jamie swooned. "I wonder what it's seasoned with."

"I'd be happy to eat all of it and let you know if I figure it out," Hyo coyly suggested.

"Not a chance." They both scooped up more of the steak and the side dishes, savoring every bite.

"Any idea who sent this to you?"

"Yeah, an old college friend named Reed. He just moved to Houston and works at an upscale restaurant that's actually not too far from here."

"Nice. He must have a crush on you." Hyo took a final bite of food.

"Nah, he's married. And we've never been anything more than friends." Jamie casually dismissed Hyo's assumption. "I'd better give him a call to thank him for the lunch." She reached for her cell phone and began to scroll through the list of contact names that were stored in the device.

"OK, I'm going to take my lunch break."

"You just ate!" Jamie quipped as she pulled up Reed's phone number at the restaurant and began to dial it on her office phone.

"That was hardly enough for an appetizer. I think that I'll go buy a cheesesteak sandwich. Do you want me to get something for you while I'm out?"

"No, thanks. I'll be full after I finish the rest of the steak. Enjoy your lunch." The phone at the restaurant began to ring. Upon someone answering, Jamie asked for Reed, who quickly took the call.

"Jamie! Did you get the package I sent to you?"

"Hey, Reed." She smiled into the phone. "Yes, my assistant and I ate most of it within five minutes. I have a little more of the steak to polish off as soon as we hang up. It was all really good. Thanks for sending it over."

"Five minutes? Wow! You two must've been starving."

"Yeah, but it wasn't enough for two, so my assistant left to get more food."

"It wasn't intended for two, but since two people partook of the meal and you've shared your opinion about it, can you tell me what your assistant thought?"

"He agreed with me that it was delicious. Why?"

"Awesome! I'm testing a few ideas for dishes that we may add to the menu, and I needed to get an objective opinion. I haven't had time to meet very many people in Houston outside of the restaurant, and I knew that you'd be brutally honest if you hated it."

"Oh! I was wondering why you would send food to me. I was going to ask if you were trying to fatten me up."

"Well, you could use a little extra meat on your bones, but I'll let Ken worry about that," he joked.

"No comment." Jamie genially shook her head. "Hey, I was going to call you today about something else. I have a favor to ask."

"All right, ask away."

"My sister is a phenomenal cook, but she doesn't have any formal culinary training like you do. Are you open to giving her a chance at one of the sous chef jobs that you mentioned the other day? She's a hard worker, and I think she'd be an asset to you."

"What's she doing right now?"

Jamie hesitated since a cashier job was a far cry from working in a restaurant kitchen. "She's a cashier at Walmart."

"Walmart? Why is she working there if she's interesting in being a sous chef?"

"To be honest with you, she wasn't thinking about being a sous chef until I mentioned your potential opening to her over the weekend. It just makes sense for her since she loves to cook. And she also has a lot of recipe ideas that she experiments with like you do. She made some baby carrots with honey and orange juice over the weekend, and I couldn't believe how good they were. So I thought about you and the restaurant. She could really use the break." It was the best sales pitch that Jamie could give since she was less than an amateur in the kitchen and had no real knowledge about what qualifications might appeal to Reed or any other professional chef.

"I'm not hiring any sous chefs yet. You were at the restaurant last week and saw how slow it is right now. My plan is to hire a couple of sous chefs when business starts to pick up."

"Oh." Jamie's disappointment was apparent in her voice. "OK, well, I just thought that I'd ask."

Reed was silent for a few moments. "Tell you what, bring your sister to the restaurant on Saturday morning at around nine o'clock. And tell her to come prepared to cook her best dish on site so that I can test her skills. If she's any good, I'll give her a shot at temporarily replacing one of the sous chefs who's going on maternity leave in a couple of weeks. I wasn't planning to bring anyone in, but I'll make an exception for a friend."

"Reed, thank you. I really do appreciate that."

"Don't thank me yet. If she can't cook, she might leave with her feelings hurt." He chuckled.

"Understood, but I doubt it." Jamie was elated, as well as confident in Layla's talents. "We'll see you on Saturday morning. And thanks again for lunch."

"No problem. Thanks to you and your assistant for being my guinea pigs."

When Jamie hung up the phone, she heaved a sigh of relief and gratitude for Reed. Had he been standing before her at that very moment, she would have given him the most crushing, appreciative hug of his life.

While the sights around San Francisco were not as enticing as their primal inclinations, Ken and Jamie did finally manage to leave their hotel after much aggravation about doing so. The October weather was a little brisk for Jamie, who promptly buttoned her sweater once they stood on the city streets together. But everything else about the day was perfect so they undertook their first mission, which was to board a cable car and get lost in the city's hills. The scenery was so beautiful, so unlike the flat terrain in Houston, that Jamie was both enamored and awestruck as they rode up and down the boundless peaks.

"If my family wasn't in Houston, I'd move here," she said to Ken without taking her eyes off of the landscape. "It's so beautiful."

"It's nice, but I don't think I could live here. The cost of living is too high."

"That is definitely true. California and New York are both expensive."

"But I could live in New York."

"Then you're a hypocrite about California."

"Yeah, maybe so," he smirked. "I guess I just like New York."

"Why? The winters there are horrible, and the people are rude."

"The people are the reason I like it. They're real. They say what they mean, and that's a good way to be."

"So you'd live there and pay two thousand dollars a month to rent a five-hundred-square-foot apartment?"

"Maybe." He chuckled and looked at Jamie. "Have you ever been to New York?"

"No."

"Then how do you know that New Yorkers are rude?"

"I've met some New Yorkers."

"Were they rude to you?"

"Well, no, but I've heard—"

"Have I ever told you that my mother is from New York? And she's the sweetest woman you'll ever meet. But she'll also tell you like it is. She's not pretentious like a lot of southerners, who worry about being all polite in your face while they're stabbing you in the back."

Jamie knew exactly what Ken meant, more so now than when he had made the comment over one month ago. Thanks to Jacob, she was living the bedlam of having someone smiling in her face while smearing her name behind closed doors. She was scheduled to meet with her sneaky foe today, and Jamie had vainly hoped to have some ammunition against him by now. But she still had nothing, leaving her with no choice but to question him with crossed fingers that he might inadvertently reveal a hint at where the Postern product had gone awry. She was warily waiting for him when he arrived at her office.

"I've been looking forward to talking to you ever since you set up this meeting," Jacob stated as he loped to a chair situated in front of Jamie's desk. "We haven't had a chance to talk as much as we used to, and I've missed our chats."

"The end of the year is always the busiest time for my team. Hard to believe that Christmas is right around the corner, huh?" Jamie did her best to camouflage her angst and her disdain for his company. Enduring their customary small talk was now a form of torture to her.

"It sure is! I've been lazy about getting the shopping done. Luckily, my wife has been dropping all kinds of hints about what she wants me to buy her, so at least I don't have to guess about that." He snickered. "Happy wife, happy life. All smart married men abide by that rule."

"Good, good." Fully disinterested in Jacob's jibber jabber, Jamie pushed copies of a few reports across the desk for him to reference. "We've only got thirty minutes, so let's get down to business. As you know, I called this meeting to talk about the Postern revenue shortfall."

Jacob stiffened slightly as he picked up the reports. "Right, we've definitely got a problem there."

"Yes, we do." She pointed to the cliff-like revenue decline depicted on the first graph that she and Ken had discussed last week. "I know that Ivan has already spoken to several people in your team about researching the causes for the sharp declines that we can see in this graph. And we're already looking into several potential factors that would lead to the drop-off, but I thought that we should also get any insights that you might have."

"Sure, I'm happy to help if I can."

"Great. For starters, you may recall that Ivan and I went over all of the assumptions with you and Alfredo before we finalized the revenue projections earlier this year."

"Yep, I remember that meeting."

"This morning I spent a few hours revisiting those assumptions and saw that they all held up for the first two months after the product was launched. And then an unexpected volume of customers began to drop the product. That's represented by the revenue-declination trend that we begin to see here." She pointed to the cliff.

"Right, I've seen this graph." Jacob was keeping his responses quite clipped, which was exactly the opposite of what Jamie had hoped for. The more he talked, the more likely he was to expose information that she believed in her gut he was hiding from both her and Tom.

"Have you thought about why the customers may be dropping out of the program?"

"Sure, I've thought about it, but I'm just as baffled as everyone else. I was hoping that your team could help us out since everything on our side is running like a well-oiled machine."

"Has anyone surveyed the borrowers who are dropping out? Is there a particular complaint that keeps bubbling up when the customers call in?"

"I've heard some general complaints that their bills are too high."

"We're already looking into some potential causes for that sort of issue. It might be due to unusual spikes in the customers' kilowatt usage, but even if that's the case, the rates in the third month of the contract are still lower than the market average. So it still doesn't make sense for customers to drop the product and to even switch their service away from Radian."

"I know. That's what my team has been telling customer service when they pass on the complaints to us." Jacob remained cool and maintained eye contact with Jamie. If he was hiding anything, his duplicity was impossible for her to detect. "Actually, I was wondering if the problem was some sort of billing issue. Has Ivan looked into that?"

"Billing? Why would that be a problem?"

"I don't know. Maybe the customers are being overcharged?"

"How can they be overcharged when they're being charged based on their contracts?"

"Maybe the meter reads reported for their bills are incorrect. I'm just thinking out loud since the customers are saying that their bills are too high."

"But we already have plenty of protocols in place to protect customers from that sort of thing. I don't think that the problem is related to the meters." The fact was that it was virtually impossible for an erroneous meter read to occur since most of those processes had been automated and an external entity performed a series of routine audits.

"I could be way off," Jacob acknowledged. "Again, I'm just thinking out loud since you asked for my insight. I definitely don't think that the issue is how the product is structured. We picked all of that apart before the launch. So the problem has to be something external to the structure, which is where your team comes in."

Jacob seemed all too smug for Jamie's liking. Even worse, he had successfully avoided making any statements that she could pounce on. She silently mulled over his last statement, a veiled but obvious swing at her competence. He certainly was sure of himself. And so was she. She would stake her life on the fact that someone outside of her team—most likely the man sitting before her now—was responsible for the Postern problem. To cover all the bases, she would ask Ivan to confirm that each customer's kilowatt-hour usage was reported accurately in their billing system, although the probability of errors was nearly zero.

"Your point about potential billing errors is interesting. I'll speak with Ivan about whether we have any problems there." Jamie was openly doubtful.

"I think you should. But if the problem isn't related to kilowatt-hour billing errors, I've gotta tell ya, I really don't know what it could be." Jacob stood up to leave with a concerned look. "If I can do anything to help you figure this thing out, let me know. We're a team, and I've got your back."

"Thanks, I appreciate that." Jamie would have loved to discuss the knife that he had already planted in her back, but that would accomplish nothing.

He reached her door and paused. "You mentioned in this morning's meeting that your team is working to wrap up the research by next Friday, right?"

"That's the plan."

"OK, great. We're all looking forward to getting this thing resolved and behind us." He opened the door before yet another thought occurred to him. "We should do lunch this week so that we can catch up on other things unrelated to work like we used to. I think that I'm open tomorrow. How about you?"

Jamie had no intention of being marooned with Jacob for any reasons that she could control. "Let's play it by ear. I have a lot of irons in the fire right now."

"Sure. I'll check with you in the morning." His smile was again too smug as he exited the office. If he was in some way responsible for the revenue problem, he was also satisfied that he had covered his tracks too well for Jamie to find them.

Deflated, Jamie sulked for a few moments. Jacob was proving to be a slick adversary, and she didn't like feeling as though he had the upper hand. Before she could begin to stew, she forced herself to get up and out of her office. She needed to move around, the idea being that movement might help to clear her mind. Upon reaching the corridor, she happened to spot Ken leaving the printing room, and she reflexively halted. All of his attention was concentrated on the documents in his hands as he walked back to his office. For an instant, Jamie considered taking a detour so she could talk to him. She knew that she could trust him with how she was feeling about the Postern fiasco as well as her suspicions about Jacob. But his new attitude toward her that morning kept her frozen in place. Something told her that he would eviscerate her if she entered his lair. And she had great faith in her instincts. For now, she had to let this sleeping dog lie. But before she could continue with her much-needed walk, she saw Chantal intercept Ken outside of his office. He immediately gave her that disarming smile that Jamie knew so well and began chatting with the woman, who seemed to be prancing and posing to display all of the body parts that were barely concealed beneath her tight dress. It seemed that Katrina was right again. Short of performing a striptease, Chantal was doing everything possible to scintillate Ken's curiosity.

Jamie felt a renewed pounding in her chest as she watched Chantal press something into Ken's hand before finally walking away. He gazed at whatever it was as he moseyed into his office, leaving Jamie to wonder what Chantal had given him. Was it her phone number? Maybe a photo of some sort? Katrina had said that Chantal planned to pull out all of the stops to get Ken's attention. For the first time, Jamie now wondered what that meant.

# CHAPTER 9

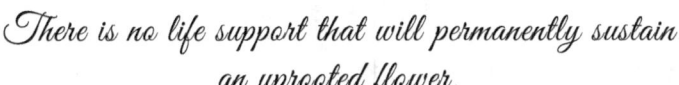

*There is no life support that will permanently sustain an uprooted flower.*

THE ROSES WERE dead. After a valiant two-week fight for precious life in sunless rooms, they had finally succumbed to their inevitable fate, withering to nothing more than dried black scraps that looked more like burnt paper. It seemed fitting, Jamie thought, since the condition of the flowers mimicked the condition of her relationship with Ken. It was over. Not long ago, she would have said that it had never started, so if he chose to be remote now, to treat her as if she were practically a stranger, that was fine with her. She was accustomed to having distance between them, and his coldness of late merely served to maintain that to which she was accustomed. And this was exactly what she wanted. Right?

Jamie took the brittle, dead roses and held them over the trash can, relieved that they would finally be out of her house and her sight once and for all. She was glad that she could inhabit her home once more without the intrusive blooms. But before she released them, she hesitated. She had never wanted them, had resented their invasive presence, and yet strangely enough, she was a little sad at tossing them out like so many other useless, undesirable things. She couldn't help wondering if the thorns were still as merciless as they had been when the roses were fresh and bright. Upon pressing the tip of her finger against one, the question was rapidly answered—it still hurt like hell. Time had not dulled their capacity to stab like tiny knives. This time, she didn't hesitate when she held them over the trash can. But that pang of sadness was still there when she dropped them in. She stood over them for a long moment, looking down at the black, withered petals. They had not deserved her cruel treatment. She knew that. But there was no bringing them back now.

Feeling an inexplicable languor, Jamie reflected on the flowers as she accompanied Layla to her cooking trial at Pazmeel later that morning. They had already left Sadie and Luke with their mother, who seemed happy enough without any meddlesome flowers in her life. Mama stayed busy with her siblings, her grandchildren, and her long-time friends from church. There were no flowers to be found anywhere. So why were flowers such a big deal? Was she destined for devastation if she never received another flower?

As Jamie pondered her possible life, Layla seemed to be on the verge of escaping her personal lion's den, prattling excitedly all the way to the restaurant while Jamie mooned, feeling helpless and confused. Not wanting to spoil her sister's euphoria, Jamie tried to listen as Layla described the dish she was planning to cook for Reed and how she had decided that it was the perfect dish to prove her skills to the chef. At times, a handful of Layla's comments seeped through Jamie's preoccupation, at which point she muttered as if she had actually heard everything that Layla said.

When they arrived at the restaurant, Reed animatedly greeted them at the front door, let them in, and locked the door behind them to prevent any wayward customers from entering by accident. The restaurant didn't open for business until lunchtime, which meant that, with the exception of two sous chefs who were already prepping various meats and vegetables for the lunch menu, Layla would have the kitchen to herself.

"I would never guess that you two are sisters," Reed remarked after showing Layla around the kitchen, approving the dish that she planned to prepare, and leaving her to her work. "You look nothing alike."

Reed and Jamie seated themselves at the exact same table where they had sat last week. Only this time, the dining area was vacant save for a few waiters readying the tables for the sparse lunch traffic. Unable to abstain from her own gloom, yet another uncomplimentary word to describe the dining-room area occurred to Jamie—lifeless.

"I know. She looks like our dad, and I look like our mom."

"She seems like a nice lady. And she's really lucky to have you for a sister because she wouldn't be in my kitchen right now if it weren't for you." Reed chuckled.

Jamie also smiled. "Thanks again for giving her this chance. It means a lot to both of us."

"It's the least that I can do since you taste tested some of my dishes this week." Reed had sent more free lunches to Jamie, taking care to add a second helping of everything for Hyo now that he understood that he actually had two very willing pushovers sampling the dishes.

"No problem. Between you and Layla, my diet has been healthier over the past week than over the past year. I just hope that you don't cause me to burst out of my clothes." The two friends laughed at the idea for a moment.

"So I noticed that your lip is still stuck out today. Are you and Ken still on the outs?"

"Yeah. Looks like that that ship has sailed." Jamie was immediately sullen once more and cast her eyes downward before restoring her gaze to Reed's inquisitive eyes. "What about you and Lisa?" Lisa was Reed's wife.

"'Bout the same as you and Ken, I guess. I don't hear from her unless she needs money."

They sat in silence, both wallowing in their own blues.

"The roses died." Jamie finally broke the silence.

"What roses?"

"The roses that Ken gave me last week. They were dead yesterday when I got home."

"So what?"

"So—I don't know. I don't even know why I brought them up."

"You seem upset about it. What's the big deal? They were just flowers." Reed had unwittingly echoed Jamie's own wonderings.

"That's just it. Were they just flowers? Or were they something more?"

"More like what?" Reed looked skeptically at Jamie, who sighed heavily.

"People keep telling me that when men give flowers to women, it means that they love them. But I know that that's not true because I've gotten hundreds of flowers from dozens of men who usually turned out to be sneaky, low-down scoundrels."

"Wow! Were they really that bad?"

"Yes. Trust me, I am not exaggerating."

"But you know something? That says to me that you have bad taste in men. You're the one who keeps picking these duds. And they can't date you without your cooperation, right?"

Jamie thoughtfully considered Reed's opinion for a moment, looking for holes in his reasoning. There seemed to be none. Her depression immediately deepened.

"No, I guess not."

"I'm not trying to bust you down, but it just sounds like you're a big part of your own problem. You've probably met some good guys over the years who would've treated you the way you want to be treated, but you weren't interested in them. Like me, for example."

"Huh?" Jamie's head snapped up so she could look at Reed, reflexively recoiling with unease at the same time.

"Me, Jamie. I had a huge crush on you in college. But I didn't have that slick quality that you seemed to like. You were more interested in that Slim Dawg character who was chasing everything on campus in a skirt."

"You were my friend, Reed. More like a big brother, really."

"I know that. Believe me, I know. But I had hoped that we'd be more than that."

Jamie frowned, still feeling guarded. "I'm sorry, Reed. You're right. I never saw you that way."

"I understand. I wasn't bad enough. I was too trustworthy and reliable."

She looked away, silently soaking in the significance of Reed's criticism. Rather than faulting the duplicitous men for their litter of deceits, Reed faulted her for inviting them into her life. She had made the choices to date them, a perspective that made her feel like a complete idiot.

"What's wrong with me? Why am I like this?" She forgot her disconcertion as she contemplated her self-sabotage.

"Don't feel too bad. You're like a lot of women out there. Y'all just go for the bad boys. But then you complain when they treat you the way you should've expected."

"But I don't want to be this way. It's stupid!"

"If you don't want to be that way, then make a choice to change. Go out with someone who you normally wouldn't give a chance. Go out with me."

Once again, Jamie's defenses shot upward and around her at his suggestion. "You? But you're married!"

Reed merely shrugged. "Not for much longer at the rate things are going."

She leapt to her feet. "Reed, I can't go out with you. I—I—" She was stumbling badly, at a loss for words.

Just then, Layla walked in with her dish and a broad grin, taking no notice of Jamie's flustered demeanor. She carefully set down a white dinner plate as Jamie released a sigh of relief at the timely interruption. For Reed's expert assessment, Layla had prepared a blackberry balsamic chicken breast, which she was clearly proud to present to him.

"Here ya go," she said as she stepped back to give Reed some space to slice and taste the chicken.

"Looks good." While Jamie was still extremely rattled, Reed had not lost a beat, seeming lucid and completely comfortable in his skin. He picked up a knife and fork and sliced a small bite-size piece and placed it in his mouth. "Oh, this is good. This is really good."

Layla's face lit up at the praise. "Thank you!"

"You've got skills. Better than I expected, to tell you the truth." Reed pushed the plate to Jamie so she could also taste the chicken, but her appetite was nonexistent.

"I'll try it later. I'm sure that it's delicious."

"So does that mean that I've got the job?" Excited, Layla's attention was only on Reed, and her voice had reached a higher pitch than normal.

"If you can start next week, it sure does."

As she had done days ago in Jamie's kitchen, Layla began to hop around happily and to clap her hands as though twenty years had suddenly been shaved off her age. "Thank you! Thank you!"

Although strained, Jamie smiled with Reed at Layla's obvious delight. "I'm glad that you're so happy." Reed stood up and walked away toward an area that he and the restaurant manager used as an office. "I need to get an application for you to fill out. Be right back."

Layla approached Jamie and hugged her sister's neck and shoulders while Jamie remained seated. "Thank you for helping me! You're the best!"

"I just asked him to give you a chance. You did the rest." Jamie could barely contain her anxiety. She was ready to get out of there.

Layla released Jamie, still overwhelmed with giddy enthusiasm. "I'll put in for a leave of absence at Walmart today since I'm just filling in for the sous chef who's taking maternity leave. But I really do hope that I never have to go back."

"Just remember—baby steps. If you do well here but Reed can't hire you permanently, he'll at least give you a reference for a different opportunity somewhere else."

"That's fine!" Layla clapped her hands together again, overjoyed at her prospective future.

Out of the corner of her eye, Jamie saw that Reed was coming back, and dread overwhelmed her. "Hey, let's wrap this up as quickly as possible. I need to get back to the house to read some reports that I brought home from the office."

"OK, sure!" At this point, Layla was so happy that she wouldn't have cared if Jamie had asked her to run naked through the restaurant.

Once again, Jamie found herself in a state of flight, this time from Pazmeel and Reed. As she and Layla headed to Mama's house to retrieve the kids, she still couldn't believe that Reed had asked her out on a date. She was appalled and offended by the idea. And the next time they spoke, she would let him know that he had crossed a line with her. She may have been dumb enough to date some pretty lousy guys, but one thing she wouldn't do is date a married man. And his overture had probably just ruined their friendship forever.

As with the drive to the restaurant earlier that morning, Jamie's moody preoccupation went unnoticed as Layla giddily chattered about her newfound cooking career all the way to Mama's house. When they pulled into the driveway and went to a side door, Jamie would have sworn on a stack of Bibles that Layla had not paused to take a single breath in the past twenty minutes.

Jamie used her key to unlock the door, and the sisters entered the house through the main living room area. Surprisingly, no one greeted them, although the television was turned on to a channel with Bugs Bunny and Elmer Fudd.

"Mama!" Jamie called out.

"Back here!" they heard her respond.

The sisters walked toward a hallway that led to the rear of the house. Typical of the schizophrenic Texas winter weather, the temperature outside had gone from the forties to the sixties within a matter of days. It was just warm enough for the kids to be outside in the backyard, burning off some energy.

They found Mama sitting in her favorite rocking chair and watching the kids play kickball through a window just inside the warm house. Jamie and Layla joined her and watched the kids for a few moments.

"How did your cooking trial go?" Mama asked Layla without averting her eyes from Luke and Sadie.

"It went great! I got the job!"

"Of course you got the job. I knew you would."

"Mama, I brought the dish that Layla cooked." Jamie had asked to take it in a doggie bag to expedite their departure. "Do you want to try it?"

"Not right now, honey, I had breakfast with the kids after you dropped them off, and I'm still full. Why don't you put it in the kitchen, and I'll try it later."

"OK." Jamie removed her jacket and went to the kitchen as Layla joined her kids in the backyard. When Jamie returned to her mother's side, they both watched Layla, Sadie, and Luke play kickball together. Although Jamie was still deeply perturbed by her conversation with Reed, she said nothing about it.

"So how is Layla doing? She says that she's looking for a new place to live without Paul."

"I know. She's got her eye on an apartment in Richmond."

"Why Richmond? That's too far out."

"I think that that's the point, Mama. Paul doesn't have any money, and she wants to make it as hard as she can for him to drop by unannounced."

"Humph! That one," was Mama's only response as she watched Layla laugh while kicking the ball toward Luke as he giggled. "Everything going OK with you? You hardly talk about yourself these days."

"Yeah, well…" Jamie had never mentioned Ken to her mother, and she didn't feel like talking about the crisis at work, which left very few topics to discuss. For the sake of Mama not feeling shut out of her life, Jamie decided to let her mother in on her exchange with Reed. "I just had the oddest conversation with Reed while Layla and I were at the restaurant. He wanted to know if I would go out with him."

"I thought you said that Reed was married now."

"He is, but he thinks he'll be getting divorced. He and his wife are having problems."

"Oh, that's too bad. I'm sorry to hear that. But he's still married, and that means that he's off-limits."

"I know that, Mama." Jamie hated Mama's unnecessary moral reminders. "I was just surprised that he asked me out at all."

The corners of Mama's lips turned up with amusement. "Why?"

"Because I've never thought of him that way."

"That boy was always sweet on you. I could tell when you were in college."

"But he was just a friend."

"You were his friend, but he always wanted more. You couldn't see it because he wasn't your type."

There it was again—her "type."

"What do you think my type is, Mama?"

"I don't know. If I did, I'd find him and introduce him to you myself." Mama chuckled as she watched Sadie try to kick the ball to Layla, but she missed badly and took off after it. "Would that make you happy? Meeting someone and settling down?"

Mama's question surprised Jamie, who wasn't sure how she felt. "I don't know. I guess I won't know unless I meet him. Why?"

"I just thought I'd ask. We've never talked about it."

Like Mama, Jamie peered in the direction of the activities in the backyard, but her mind had suddenly flown to a different, intangible place as she continued to consider Mama's question. She preferred not to think about the someday potential for marriage. But if marriage was important to her, were her choices of men making it permanently unattainable?

"You're a lot like me," Mama eventually continued. "You're independent and free-spirited. Women like us don't need to be married to enjoy our lives."

Jamie huffed. "Women like us don't know how to recognize a good man."

Mama turned to look at Jamie. "Why do you say that?"

"Because it's true. That's why I'm single; that's why you're single; that's why Layla is probably going to be single again."

"We're single because most men are sorry. The few good ones are already taken."

"You had a good man, Mama. Daddy is a good man."

"Says who?"

"Says me, Layla, and just about everybody in the family."

"Well, none of you were married to him." She shifted her gaze back to Layla and the kids.

"You never loved him."

"What are you talking about?" Now Mama looked insulted as she turned back to Jamie with a quizzical expression. "I loved your father. I wouldn't've married him if I hadn't."

Jamie crossed her arms. "You married him because you got pregnant."

"Those are just details." Mama looked toward the backyard once more. "I loved him. At least I thought I did. I tried to love him because everyone expected us to get married before you were born. So we got married."

"And if you'd never gotten pregnant, you would never have married him."

"Probably not." Mama relented. "I would've gone to college and gotten a degree in economics or math, something like that."

"Really?" Mama had never talked about the dreams that she had once had.

"Uh-huh. I wanted to be a stockbroker or maybe a financial manager. I was always good with numbers and money. If I hadn't been, your father would've bankrupted us."

Layla was now throwing the ball to the kids.

"I wish that Layla had picked a better husband for herself. When I raised you girls, my greatest wish was that you wouldn't follow in my footsteps. I wanted both of you to be happy. That's all I ever wanted."

Jamie also watched her sister, who was giggling happily as Sadie took another stab at kicking the ball to her. "Don't worry about her, Mama. She's stronger than you may realize."

"I hope so. I really do." Mama reached out, took hold of one of Jamie's hands, and squeezed it. "I'm so grateful that she has you. What a blessing that you're helping her to discover a new life for herself!"

"She's a gifted cook, but we'll have to wait and see if that's what she wants to do for a living after she gets her feet wet at the restaurant."

"At least she's got the chance."

"Yeah, she's going to be OK."

"And so will you." Mama again squeezed Jamie's hand. "Don't worry about picking the wrong men in the past. The right man will show up at the right time. That's what I've always believed."

"What if there is no right man for me?"

"You'll still be OK. You already are."

# CHAPTER 10

*A flower's beauty is as eternal as morning dew.*

"WHERE DO YOU see yourself in ten years?" Jamie asked Ken as they sat outside of an ice cream parlor in the mild, bright sunshine with two heaping cones of ice cream. It had been a very pleasant day in San Francisco. After riding a cable car for a couple of hours, they had gotten off near a shopping center to tour the area. Now they were just spectating and talking as orange, red, and white trollies sped by. Jamie had continued to marvel at the landscape so full of rolling hills and concrete.

"I see myself as an executive somewhere and socking away a lot of money so I can retire in my fifties."

"That's a young age to retire. What would you do with yourself?" She bit into her ice cream, enjoying the smooth texture on her tongue.

"Whatever I want to do. Unless I'm married with kids. If that happens, my early retirement plan will be blown to hell. I really hope to marry a woman who's pulling down some major dough, too."

"You make a family sound like a bad thing."

"It could be if I married the wrong woman. That's a scary thought." He licked his ice cream and absentmindedly watched another trolley go by.

"I know what you mean. It's so easy to convince ourselves that we've met the right person, and we get caught up in a relationship that we want to believe will last forever. But I rarely meet people who are happily married after the first five or so years."

"Me neither. One of my buddies has really got me scared because his wife gained a bunch of weight after they got married, and now he's not attracted to her anymore. He hasn't cheated yet, but I think it's inevitable. I don't want to be in his shoes one day."

"What? Married to an overweight woman?"

"No, married to a woman whose physical body is the only thing about her that interests me in the first place. There's gotta be more than that."

Jamie continued eating her ice cream while pondering Ken's point of view. This was the second time during their trip that he had alluded to lust being mistaken for love. Was he was talking about their relationship?

"So what about you? Where do you see yourself in ten years?"

"I don't know. Still working, but I don't know what else."

"Traveling? Married?"

"I really don't know. I don't think that far ahead. I just try to take everything one day at a time."

"You should start thinking about it. Your job is just a paycheck. It shouldn't be the only thing you know you want out of life."

At the time, Jamie had brushed off Ken's comment. Five weeks ago, she had known that her life was going exactly as she wanted it to. And her job was a key reason for her personal satisfaction. But now that foundation had been shaken apart as though ruptured by an earthquake. And the security she had burrowed into was suddenly stripped away, leaving her terribly exposed.

Jamie contemplated her job and the priority she had bestowed upon it in her life. Now that she was facing the real likelihood of being fired despite all of her hard work, she was beginning to feel like a fool. Her job was just a paycheck. But she had used it as a hiding place as well as a wedge between herself and men—between her and Ken, who had barely said, "Good morning," over the past nine days if they happened to cross paths. Within that time, her anger toward him had faded, being replaced by a growing feeling that she missed the man. She missed talking to him, laughing with him, making love with him. And the truth was that she could really use a friend right now. She needed to talk to someone she could trust with her concerns about her team's research into the Postern issue, ideally someone who also understood the players, the energy industry, and the criticality of the problem. Taken together, the only person she could think of was Ken. But Ken wasn't talking to her anymore.

Jamie pined as she looked out of her office window. The sun couldn't have shone more brightly, and the sky was a crisp, cloudless blue, an alluring view that had caused her thoughts to drift to her trip with Ken to San Francisco. It had been filled with both intimacy and serenity at once, the way that it had always been with them until now. And Jamie was beginning to understand exactly how intertwined their lives had become despite having lived a thousand miles apart. She was also realizing how absurd it was that they never spoke now that he was footsteps away each day at the office. He was the one person at Radian who she trusted and who would understand the bad news that Ivan had just given her—that his research had traced the Postern forecasting error directly to her team. It had been such a careless error, one so ludicrous that none of them understood how it could have happened, but it was their error nonetheless. It didn't matter that her gut continued to wail that Jacob was somehow culpable. Without proof, her instincts were as worthless as the Postern forecast had turned out to be. And Jamie needed to start thinking about how to couch her explanation of the error when she spoke to Tom later that week, a conversation that she feared would be the beginning of the end of her career at Radian.

She used her computer to check Ken's calendar and to see when they might both have time available that day. She wasn't feeling bold enough to actually schedule a meeting with him, so after finding an opening that appeared to work for them, she tensely waited, periodically checking her clock while distractedly shuffling papers on her desk and reading e-mails between meetings. When he eventually passed her office doorway on the way to his own office, her heart began to pound as she summoned the courage to initiate the first conversation that they had had in nearly two weeks. She had never before felt so nervous about talking to Ken, and her legs almost refused to support her when she stood up. But she was determined to speak with him to share her concerns, and, more important, to discover any potential for repairing their relationship.

Jamie anxiously left her office, seconds later walking into Ken's just as he was sitting down. She was feeling both overheated and clammy when she greeted him from the doorway.

"Hi." She realized that she was wringing her hands and so lowered her arms in front of her with a weak smile.

When Ken saw her, he didn't look pleased. "What's up, Jamie?" His tone of voice was detached and impersonal. And he didn't return her smile.

"I, uh—" She touched the doorknob. "Can I close the door?"

He shrugged indifferently. "Go ahead."

"Thanks." She demurely closed the door and then took a seat near his desk while also looking around the office. It was the first time she had actually come in here since Alfredo had left the company, and so far the office still appeared to be unoccupied, as Ken had not yet personalized the space with any pictures or other mementos. "I was hoping that we could talk. I—well, a lot has been happening lately, and I couldn't think of anyone else who I could trust around here."

"That's ironic." Ken leaned back in his chair and held a pen between the fingers of both of his hands.

Jamie released a long breath. "Ken, I know that you're upset about some of the things I said a couple of weekends ago, but—"

"And I know that you're upset that I took a job at Radian, and yet—ironically—I'm the only person here who you think that you can trust."

Jamie was taken aback by his rabid sarcasm. Already on the brink of hitting rock bottom, she was in no position to handle him kicking her while she was down. She chewed her lower lip, promptly doing an internal about-face and relinquishing the fervor that had carried her to his office.

"Forget it. I shouldn't have come over." More flustered than ever, she stood up and walked toward the door, wanting him to stop her, but he didn't. She didn't know if he was watching her cross the small distance to the door, but she pulled back her shoulders, an outward show of hoisting her flagging self-confidence. When she reached the door and grabbed the doorknob, she again wished that he would stop her from leaving, but Ken said nothing. And for an instant, she hated him for the way that he was treating her. As her dignity begged her to walk out and never look back, her rational self murmured that he would have treated her much differently if she had not behaved so badly. She had created this gulf between them. Without turning around to again face him, she finally said, "I think that Jacob is trying to sabotage me and my team."

"Why do you say that?" Ken's voice lacked all real interest and emotion.

"Because he's been making accusations to Tom behind my back. He says that I'm in over my head." She turned back around to see Ken's face, which remained unreadable. "I can't prove it yet, but I know that he's done something to create the Postern revenue problems and swept it under the carpet without anyone knowing about it."

"What exactly do you think he's done?"

"I don't know. But there's a reason why he's so bent on making sure I take the fall for it."

"Jamie, are you sure that you're not just looking for some kind of scapegoat? I spoke to Ivan this morning, and I already know about your team using the wrong kilowatt-hour rates in your forecast. You were way off when you calculated the revenue expectations for customers who exceeded their contracted kilowatt allotments. And your team has looked under almost every rock and found nothing to suggest any wrongdoing, whether by Jacob or anyone else. All evidence points to human error, plain and simple." Ken's disbelief sounded like a tape recording of what Jacob was probably saying to everyone except to her.

"We estimated potential excesses like we always do, but no one can predict with one hundred percent accuracy if regional climates will deviate from their normal patterns. Customers in western states had unusual spikes in their electricity usage."

"I know that, but the problem is that the forecast applied the wrong pricing rates, and those customers received larger bills than anyone estimated, which is why they started dumping the Postern product and Radian. I can't understand why Radian would even do that—bill overages at higher rates. It's just bad business."

"You're right. I agree."

"Since you agree, did you happen to tell anyone that you thought that the contract terms could cause customer attrition?"

"No. And the truth is that I don't even remember reading that language in the contract. I'm sure that if I had seen it, I would have been jumping up and down." Jamie was deeply distraught. "We've been doing these forecasts for years, and they're reviewed by at least ten people before they're finalized. How could ten people have failed to raise concerns about those contract terms? It doesn't make any sense."

"And, again, you were one of those ten people, correct?"

"Yes, yes, of course I was." Jamie paced around the area in front of his desk. "And I always follow the same steps. I check and recheck everything before approving the projections, and we've never been as wrong as we were about the Postern product."

"Well, maybe you forgot something this time."

"I'm telling you that I didn't!" Jamie stopped to clutch the top of the chair that she had briefly occupied. "There's no way that I would do that."

Ken eyed her for a few long moments, appearing to consider the possibility of her allegations. But then the apathy clouded his eyes again. "Sounds like you have a problem on your hands."

Genuinely stunned by his chilly reaction, Jamie gaped at him. "Is that all you have to say? That I have a problem? I think that I already know that."

"I hope that you figure it out before Friday. That's your deadline with Tom, right?"

Ken had very effectively reminded her that her fate didn't matter to him. Utterly thrown, Jamie released her grip on the chair and took a couple of awkward steps backward. "Yeah, Friday is the deadline."

"OK, good luck with that." Ken averted his eyes to one of his many desk drawers and pulled one of them open. "Now if you'll excuse me, I have some work to do."

Jamie was flabbergasted by how he had just dismissed her as though she was an inconvenience to him. Not only was she speechless, but she was embarrassed that she had even come to his office thinking that she would find a friend. As she watched him, Ken began to riffle through some folders as if she had already left. Humiliated, Jamie wordlessly turned and exited his office, barely making it out before hot tears stung her eyes.

"Hey, Jamie!" She heard Randall call from somewhere behind her and waved without seeing him, unable to even croak a response as she hastily bolted toward her office. Desperate to reach a safe place before the tears spilled onto her cheeks, she practically ran the short distance and almost slammed the door behind her just as the tears began to free-ly flow. She didn't know what she had expected from Ken, but the reception she had just received had certainly left no doubt that he had written her off. She didn't have a single ally who cared whether she sank or swam in the midst of her most egregious professional tsunami. How foolish she had been to think that she could lean on Ken, on the unique connection that they had shared. As it turned out, Ken had revealed a vindictive quality that had deepened her sense of isolation. And he must have relished every moment of his revenge.

For several minutes, Jamie freely cried, drowning in her troubles and her feeling of powerlessness. She allowed herself to indulge her self-pity and her fears about the muddy fate that seemed to loom before her. But eventually, as was her overriding nature, her mind began to search for an anchor that would halt her trajectory into an unknown oblivion. Her relationship with Ken was over. He had left no doubt, and she could not change that. But her career was still in her hands, and she had not reached her posi-tion at Radian by allowing herself to be a victim. With or without anyone's help or moral support, she would find a way to win as she had always done. Before she had been promoted to a vice president, Jamie's job had been that of the analytical detective that she now relied on Ivan to be. And in the name of saving her career, she was going to become that detective again today.

Jamie rallied her laser-like focus, asked Hyo to hold all of her calls for the remainder of the afternoon, and spent the next few hours applying forensic-like research skills to solving the Postern forecast crisis. She methodically read every e-mail, memo, and report about the product that had ever crossed her desk. She also recalculated the revenue forecasts as if she'd never before seen any of the information. The end result wound up pointing to exactly what Ken had said—human error. There was no way to escape this conclusion. Somehow, she and her team had all missed the error in the pricing terms, which clearly stated that kilowatt-hour overages would be billed at higher market retail rates as opposed to the much lower rates that were applied to the customers' normal electricity usage. If she hadn't researched it herself, she would never have believed that she had overlooked such foul terms, as this sort of oversight was quite uncharacteristic of her. As she was beating herself up, she heard a soft knock on the door before Hyo entered the office.

"Got another delivery for you, Jamie." He was carrying a vase that was crammed full of elegantly arranged pink and red roses. "I guess that your friend Reed is stepping up his game."

Bewildered, Jamie sedately stood and walked around the desk as Hyo set the roses down on the only corner that wasn't covered with stacks of paper. "Is there a card?"

"I don't know. I didn't see one."

She studied the perimeter around the roses, but found no customary small white envelope submerged among the buds. "I don't know who these are from, Hyo." She again looked at the flowers, now with more curiosity.

"I just assumed it must've been Reed since he's been sending lunches to us."

"Reed is just a friend."

"I don't know any guys who would give so much attention to a woman who is just a friend."

Jamie elected not to comment. Since Reed's proposition at the restaurant on Saturday, he had called a couple of times, but she had let the calls roll into voice mail. She just wasn't ready to deal with him on top of everything else that was disintegrating around her. Maybe he had sent the flowers to break the ice.

"There must be at least one hundred roses here. And this vase looks pretty expensive, too. Reed had to have spent over three hundred dollars for this bouquet."

Jamie gasped at such an extravagant cost. "You think so?"

"Yeah. I bought my girlfriend a dozen roses for her birthday last month, and it set me back thirty bucks before I even picked out the vase. I don't know what this vase cost, but I know that I couldn't have afforded it."

"Hmm..." Jamie touched the fragile rose blooms. If they had been as expensive as Hyo guessed, then they couldn't have come from Reed. He was in no position to spend so much money. And so Ken came to mind. As already illustrated, roses were more his style, although the timing for him to send them was dubious—unless he was looking for a way to apologize for his behavior earlier. And it made sense that Ken would also choose not to include a card out of concern that it might fall into the wrong hands and reveal his more personal relationship with Jamie—the relationship that she had believed was over. But maybe she had been wrong yet again. Maybe there was still a chance to undo the damage to their relationship. As Jamie contemplated this possibility, the roses suddenly gained a more sacred quality, and she blithely inhaled their ambrosial scent. "Well, I doubt that Reed sent them."

"I don't. It's obvious that he's got a thing for you." Hyo's perceptive observation once again cast a shadow upon the roses' appeal in Jamie's mind. "By the way, I'm almost finished with the updates to the procedure manual. I should have it on your desk by tomorrow morning."

"Thank you, Hyo. I appreciate that." Jamie's gaze remained fixed on the flowers as Hyo headed back to the office door and walked out. But before he could close it behind him, Ken dashed past him without warning.

"Jamie, I was thinking about our conversation earlier and—" Ken stopped short, having noticed the roses so prominently placed on her desk. "What's this?" He walked directly toward the roses and Jamie, whose head had shot upward with hopeful surprise at the sound of his voice.

"I don't know. I thought that you might be able to tell me."

"Tell you what?"

"Did you send them?"

"Jamie, you know that I didn't send these to you," he responded with suspicion. "Why would I send flowers to a woman who just told me to get lost? I don't have to beg for a woman's attention."

"If you didn't send them, then I don't know who did. And I didn't tell you to get lost."

"Yeah, you did. You had every chance to say that you wanted to keep seeing me, but you blew me off. And now I know why. I think we both know who sent you these flowers."

"Who?" Jamie couldn't have been more baffled.

"Randall. I've seen the way he looks at you in meetings. And Katrina told me that he's been chasing you for years. I guess he caught you, but nobody knows that. Just like you didn't want anyone to know about me."

"Are you kidding me? Randall is a driveling oaf! You're the one with the secret office romance. I heard about you and Chantal."

"What does Chantal have to do with anything?"

"Katrina told me that she's planning to jump your bones. And I wouldn't be surprised if she already has. She practically molested you in the hallway the other day. I saw it with my own two eyes!"

"I don't want Chantal. That girl ain't even right in the head. I heard that she hit on her fiancé's best man a week before the wedding. Why would I want to be with a woman like that?"

"It wasn't his best man; it was his best friend. And you like her because she's an easy lay, and that's all you want anyway."

"Jamie, you're crazy. And you're listening to Katrina too much."

"Look who's talking! Randall? Puh-*lease*!"

"Maybe you're not sleeping with Randall, but it's obvious that you're sleeping with somebody. Men don't send flowers for no reason. All that talk about working late and reading reports on the weekends was just a charade. You've got another man out here, and you've been playing both of us."

"Ken, that's just not true. You're way off."

"God, I'm so stupid! I actually believed that you were working hard at your job when you didn't have time to talk to me, but the truth was that you were working hard, all right—on some other man!" Ken stared at her with an expression of profound disbelief.

"Ken, listen to me! You're wrong!"

"Yeah, OK, sure." He glared at Jamie, seething with hatred that was almost tangible. "And to think that I came in here to offer my help to you with the Postern research. I felt sorry for you, and I wanted to apologize for the way that I had treated you when you came to my office."

"I'm telling you the truth. Why won't you listen to me?"

"I'm done listening to you. You're on your own with your Postern problem." Ken stormed to the door, turning once more before exiting. "I hope that you appreciate those roses more than the ones that I gave you."

For the second time that day, tears stung Jamie's eyes as Ken charged out and she tried to comprehend what had happened. How could such a simple misunderstanding have led to even more confusion? It was as though she was living someone else's nightmare.

"Hey, what was that all about?" Having overheard some or all of the heated exchange between Ken and Jamie, a confused Hyo had poked his face back in the doorway after Ken had torn out of the office.

Inconsolably saddened, Jamie had nothing to say. She merely waved her hand weakly, gazed miserably at the roses and then humbly at the floor.

"Are you OK?" He sounded concerned.

She nodded, still saying nothing.

"Are you sure?"

She nodded again, her eyes glued to the floor near her feet.

"Do you want me to close the door?"

She nodded.

"OK. If you need anything, just let me know, OK?"

Once again, the faintest of nods comprised her response.

Hyo obediently closed the door, at which point Jamie placed both of her hands over her face and wept uncontrollably, her chest heaving as though there wasn't enough air in the room to fill her lungs. She felt like she had literally been ejected from her life. And the pressure of everything that was coming at her from so many different directions was finally causing her to buckle.

Through severely blurred vision, she found her way to her chair and dropped herself down with little grace. The self-pity that she had earlier managed to fend off had rematerialized in full force and finished off her remaining reserves of resilience. But it probably didn't matter anyway since all of her research that afternoon had led to Ivan's same conclusion. Her team had made the forecasting error, which meant that everything she had worked so hard to attain at Radian would soon be reduced to smoke. She had wanted to believe that her many accomplishments at the company had rendered her invincible, but the truth was that the accomplishments were fickle trophies that had no long-term value to anyone except her. In the end, regardless of the number of trophies that she amassed, she was alone. And being alone meant being stronger than she could possibly be all of the time.

Jamie swiveled her chair around so that she was facing her window, the window through which she had watched so many beautiful sunsets and reminded herself to think big. She had been convinced that lofty ideas brought about ideal results, as thinking big was supposed to spur the best outcomes. But thinking big was no longer working for her. In fact, thinking big had brought her to a place that she now recognized was a mirage. And that mirage had just vanished before her eyes, leaving her immobilized, broken with a sunset before her that no longer provided a shred of solace. Today there would be no comfort found in any heavenly view. Instead, she was confronted with her own failings—and her undesired solitude.

# CHAPTER 11

*A blooming flower would be happier unseen if it thus is not plucked.*

WHEN JAMIE ARRIVED at her house late that night, she could barely drag herself from her car to the back door, passing sluggishly through the utility room with the enigmatic roses in hand. While she still wasn't certain who had sent them, it was clear that Ken could be crossed off the list. Luckily, the list was hardly extensive, leading Jamie to assume that Reed must have sent the roses as Hyo had deduced. Reed wanted a chance that she couldn't imagine giving to him. Not only was he married, but he simply did not interest her romantically. Maybe, as he asserted, he was too nice, too good a man to ignite her *amore*. And, if so, did that mean that Ken was actually another bad boy? The questions were endlessly circular, running into each other and taking her nowhere.

In this moment, she didn't like herself. And she didn't understand herself. But one thing she did understand was that she definitely didn't want the roses she carried now that she knew that Ken had not sent them. They meant nothing to her. Still, she would be gracious this time. She would thank Reed for his thoughtfulness and be sure to clear up any ambiguity that they could ever be more than friends—and even that was questionable.

She entered her living room expecting to see Layla but instead found her father sitting on the sofa, watching television with Bear on his lap.

"Hello, stranger. Long time no see." He stood up to walk around the sofa.

"Hey, Daddy." Her mood was immediately lifted as she hugged him. "I'm sorry that I haven't been by in a couple of weeks. I've been really busy at work. You know how it is." Unlike Mama, Daddy lived on the outskirts of Houston with his wife of twenty years, Valerie. The drive to his house was around one hour, which was like driving to a different city altogether. Jamie set down her purse and car keys, but not the roses since she had decided to place them in the last spare bedroom, out of sight.

"I know how you are. You're very dedicated to your job." He glanced at the roses. "And from the looks of it, you've been dedicated to something else as well."

"No, Daddy, it's not like that." Jamie smiled thinly. "Where's Layla?"

"Someone at the restaurant called in sick, and she volunteered to cover for the person. Luckily, I was able to pick up the kids from school and get Layla's house key from her. She's so happy about that job that I couldn't let her down."

"That was really kind of you."

"I'm not being kind. She's my daughter, and her children are my grandchildren. Of course I'll help when I can."

"You made a long drive, though, Daddy. And now it's late. I don't want you on the road, trying to drive back home at this hour."

"I don't plan to. My old eyes get tired, and I don't see as well at night, so I brought some things with me. They're already in the bedroom."

"OK, that's good. And what about the kids? Are they already in bed?"

"I put 'em to bed at nine o'clock. And Layla asked me to feed Bear if you weren't home by five o'clock."

"Thank you, Daddy." Jamie yawned and used her empty hand to cover her mouth. "I'm worn out, so I'm going to bed now. It's really been a long day."

"I understand. You get some rest. I don't sleep as many hours as I did when I was as young as you, so I'm gonna watch a little TV. You have a good night."

"You, too." She pecked his cheek and walked toward her bedroom with the roses in hand and Bear trailing closely behind her. Now that Daddy was occupying the last guest room, she considered leaving the roses in the kitchen or the mudroom but then decided that it didn't matter one way or the other where they were. Soon enough, they would be in the garbage can, where they belonged.

Jamie was hurting more than she could remember ever before hurting. Whether her eyes were wide open or closed, all she could see was Ken's condemning glare as she mentally replayed the scene at the office. It was as though they were strangers to each other. But maybe it was for the best. If her track record was any gauge, he was just another heartbreak waiting to happen anyway. She reasoned all of this to herself as she lay in bed. The problem with all of this reasoning, though, was that her head wasn't talking to her heart, which was woefully mangled. Somehow, at some point, she had fallen in love without realizing it. Ken the toy had turned into Ken the man. Whether or not he was a good man was the most nebulous unanswered question. But now, as with the latest vase of roses, it didn't matter.

"Damn!" Jamie rolled over in bed and stared at the wall without seeing it. She thought about the roses that she suspected were from Reed and asked herself if she could ever love him. Could Reed ever stir her to feel for him the way she felt for Ken? Without question, the answer was a resounding *no*. Ken had managed to do something that Jamie had thought was impossible. He had actually sneaked into her heart through an imperceptible crack. And now there he was, looking back at her from inside of her as she faced the wall. She held her pillow closer and re-membered how it felt to hold Ken close, clutching it as she had Ken's body not so long ago in San Francisco. After a day spent riding trolleys and snapping photos of the Golden Gate Bridge, they had planned to cap the evening with a midnight swim on Saturday night. But yet again they had instead held each other captive in their hotel room. Jamie had emerged from the bedroom in a bathing suit cover-up that barely concealed the skimpy bikini she was wearing beneath it and unthinkingly set off a chain reaction that started with Ken's warm, soft lips on her neck followed by his tongue tickling her skin between the kisses. Soon, he had pulled her to the sofa near the patio that overlooked the ocean just beyond their window and tugged her down until she was sitting on his lap, straddling him and rolling her head backward to make every inch of her skin accessible to his lips. Jamie remembered how quickly she had begun to crave the intoxicating heat of his firm body against her own, how the urgent caress of his hands on her thighs had nearly driven her mad as he pulled loose her bikini straps. They had planned to go swimming at the hotel pool that night, but they had wound up swimming in each other instead. And Jamie had stood on the edge of love's pool when he had pressed his body deeply into hers, wiping out everything except the feel of him against and inside of her, taking her to a dimension that he alone ruled and where he commanded her very being.

As she relived the memories, Jamie buried her face in the velvety soft fabric of her pillow, allowing herself to be there in San Francisco again, but this time she did one thing differently—she expressed her feelings to Ken the way she should have done then. She should have listened to the emotions that had been whispering to her heart and shared them despite the risk. Layla was right. Jamie was absolutely terrified of Ken, of what he provoked inside her. But more than that, she was terrified of the life she would lead without him. Her fear, not Ken, had proven to be her enemy.

Lost in her abyss of reverie and loss, she barely heard the knock on her door. Daddy wanted to know if she wanted any breakfast. Jamie rubbed her eyes and turned to look at her clock. It was nearly seven o'clock. And she should already be getting dressed for work if she were going to make it to the office on time without a death-defying rush. But Jamie already knew that she wasn't going in today. She just couldn't face the unpleasant reality—the dust cloud—that awaited her there. And there was no doubt that it would still be waiting for her if she put off confronting it until tomorrow.

She also didn't feel like lugging herself out of bed, but Daddy had already made breakfast, and Jamie couldn't disappoint him. She reluctantly agreed to the meal and then called work to leave a message on Hyo's voice mail. She was taking a sick day and needed all of today's meetings rescheduled. While Jamie couldn't claim a physical malady, she could certainly say that she was suffering from an oppressive bout of mental weariness.

Not long after leaving the message for Hyo, Jamie lethargically wandered out of her bedroom, let Bear out into the backyard, and shuffled into the kitchen to prepare a plate of unwanted food.

"You're not going into the office today?" Daddy was already fully dressed in jeans and a neat button-down shirt.

"No, I called in sick." Jamie retrieved a clean plate that Daddy had already placed on the counter. With a mug of steaming coffee in hand, he watched as she placed eggs, bacon, and toast on her plate. He couldn't cook fancy dishes, but he could handle the simple ones well enough.

"Are you feeling OK?"

"Yeah, I'm OK. Just tired." She got a fork, walked to the dining-room table, sat down, and slouched in her chair, her depression encumbering every thought and movement. Daddy didn't miss a single gesture and seemed a little worried.

"Are you sure that you're not sick? You look like something is wrong." He got the carton of orange juice from the refrigerator and poured a glass for Jamie. "Here, drink this. The vitamin C will do you good."

"Thank you, Daddy." Jamie didn't want the orange juice, but she began to drink it to make him happy as he continued to watch her with conspicuous concern.

Jamie had placed a tiny piece of toast in her mouth and was starting in on the eggs when Layla walked into the house, having just dropped off her kids at school.

"I'm back! Is breakfast still hot?" She immediately went into the kitchen and got a plate to pile food onto.

"It sure is. Help yourself." Daddy refilled his mug of coffee and then took a seat at the dining-room table near Jamie as Layla prepared her plate. "What's going on with you, Jamie? You don't seem to be sick. You seem to be down."

She stopped the pretense that she was going to eat much of anything on her plate and raised her eyes to her father's. "I hate my life."

Layla joined them at the table with a mountain of food on her plate and immediately dug in.

"Why?" Daddy's brow creased. "I thought that everything was going well for you. What's happened?"

"What's wrong, Jamie?" Layla bit into a strip of bacon while eying her sister curiously but without any real concern.

"I just can't do anything right. Everything that I thought was going well is falling apart around me. It's all out of control, and I don't know what to do."

"Slow down, baby girl, slow down, and tell me what happened." Even though Layla was actually the "baby girl" in the family, Daddy routinely referred to both of his daughters as his baby girls.

Jamie shook her head despondently and released a long breath. "I'm probably going to be fired from my job, and it's possible that I've run off the first genuinely good man I've ever dated. And I ran him off because I didn't want him. But then again, I do actually want him. I just didn't realize it until he stopped wanting me. At the end of the day, I think it's OK, though, because he was probably just another jerk with a big, bad secret since I have a pattern of picking the absolutely worst men on planet Earth anyway. That's everything in a nutshell."

Both Daddy and Layla had done their best to follow Jamie's tirade. While Layla understood enough about Jamie's history with Ken to also understand the problem, Daddy looked terribly confused.

"Let's talk about one problem at a time," he suggested. "Why are you about to lose your job?"

"Because I made a mistake—a horrible, horrible mistake that is already costing the company millions of dollars. Everyone, including me, thought that I could virtually walk on water, but as it turns out, I can't. So I'm pretty sure that I'll be pounding the pavement to find a new job as early as next week."

At this revelation, Layla had stopped eating. "Jamie, you never mentioned any of this to me." Now her level of concern visibly exceeded their father's.

"That's because I thought I had it under control. I couldn't believe that I had screwed up so badly, but I've had to accept that I did. Jamie Dubois messed up big-time, and I have to tell my boss in two days."

"Oh, Jamie, that's awful!" Layla touched Jamie's shoulder sympathetically. "I wish that I could do something to help you."

"I do, too." Daddy tried to comfort her. "But maybe it won't be as bad as you think. Your boss must know by now that you are the best of the best and he's lucky to have someone as hardworking as you."

"Daddy, I'm supposed to save the company money. That's a big part of my job. If I can't do that, I'm useless to him."

"I know how important this job is to you. Maybe if you tell him—"

"I'm just going tell him the facts." Jamie cut Layla off. "If he fires me, I'll accept that and move on." She looked at both Layla and her father. "I've let my job take over my life. You said it yourself, Layla. I've treated my job like it's my man. I shouldn't've done that. It's just a job, right? And ultimately, I'm expendable."

Layla now looked bewildered as she leaned back against her chair.

"If they fire you, they're crazy!" Daddy's pride in Jamie surged.

"Thanks, Daddy. But maybe I needed this wake-up call, bad as it is. I've been using my job to avoid emotions that I didn't want to deal with, and now I don't have a choice. My cover is blown, and I can see that I've got some serious issues."

"Is this about the man you want or don't want or...I couldn't understand what you were saying. Which is it?"

"It's the man I didn't want but who I might've been wrong about, in which case I do want him, but he doesn't want me."

Daddy looked over at Layla. "Did you get that?"

"She's talking about Ken, Daddy. She met him earlier this year."

"Oh, I see. Ken. Got it. You haven't told me about this one."

"I haven't told hardly anyone about him because I wasn't taking the relationship seriously. He was just, I don't know, something to do. Someone to go out with every once in a while."

"But you fell for him?" Daddy was working to put the pieces together.

Jamie only nodded in response to his question.

"I told the girl that he was going to head for the hills after the way she talked to him." Layla crossed her arms and her legs. "I told her she'd better be sure she wanted that."

"So now you're going to rub it in, huh?" Jamie threw her hands into the air in disbelief.

"No, I'm just saying that you gave him no choice. I knew that you liked him more than you were saying, but you were too stubborn to admit it."

"Well, I'm admitting it now, OK? I screwed up! I screwed up my job, and I screwed up my love life!"

"Hold on, you two. I need to make sure that I've got this straight. Jamie, you didn't want this Ken person, but then you changed your mind after you ran him off?"

"Right."

"Baby girl, I'm sorry to break this to you, but you might be a little bit crazy like your mama."

Jamie and Layla exchanged looks before Layla burst into laughter as Daddy smirked.

"OK, Daddy, ha-ha, very funny," Jamie responded without humor. "I probably am a little crazy, but it was men who made me this way, not Mama."

"Men like who? That Julius who you used to bring around?"

"All of them! They've all driven me crazy. But you know what? I'm going to take my power back. My friend Reed thinks that I'm my own problem because I pick sorry men."

"I always did like Reed. He had a crush on you when y'all were in college, ya know."

"I know, I know. Reed told me; Mama's told me. Everybody knew except me."

"Reed has a crush on you?" Layla nearly spilled her mug of coffee.

"He had a crush on her fifteen years ago," Daddy clarified for her.

"And he's still got a crush on me now, according to him. But that's a no go because he's married, and he's not my type."

"He won't be married for long if what I'm hearing at the restaurant is true. He and his wife argue every time she calls."

"It doesn't matter."

"That's right. And you know what? I've changed my mind. I don't like Reed. Stay away from him."

"Don't worry about me, Daddy. I can handle him." Jamie paused introspectively. "But I do think he's right. I always pick the bad boys. Why is that? Why wasn't I attracted to Reed in college?"

"Because he wasn't a challenge, and you've always liked challenges," Layla diagnosed. "You're the same way with your job. You wouldn't enjoy it if it was too easy."

"But am I so deranged when it comes to men that I'm masochistic? I just can't fall for a guy who happens to worship the ground I walk on?"

"No," Layla quickly responded. "You can't. He'd bore you to tears."

"Then I was right. I've got some serious issues!"

"Don't get carried away. There's nothing wrong with enjoying a challenge, but you can't allow that quality to wreak so much havoc in your personal life."

"How do I do that, Daddy? By forcing myself to go out with someone I wouldn't throw water on if he was on fire?"

"By paying attention to yourself and learning from your mistakes. We all have to do it. After I married your mama, I just knew that I had married the devil incarnate. And you can believe that I wasn't going to make that mistake again. Before I married Valerie, I evaluated that woman and our compatibility for three years. And didn't even think about proposing until I knew I wouldn't be jumping back into the fiery pits of hell."

This time, Jamie couldn't help laughing at her father's hyperbole despite having heard his opinion of Mama countless times. Her thoughts drifted to the comment that Ken had once made about being afraid to marry the wrong woman. She hadn't considered that his fear was probably fairly common among men, especially those who had already been burned. Of course, Jamie had been burned scores of times as well, just not while married to the offender.

"Daddy, I'm taking that advice!" Layla stood up to get more coffee. Like Jamie, she had hardly put a dent in her breakfast, which had to be ice cold by now.

"You've always been hard on yourself. Ever since you were a little girl, you expected yourself to be perfect." Daddy smiled at Jamie.

"I know."

"But you don't have to be perfect. No one expects that of you. We're all proud of you."

"I know, Daddy." Jamie shrugged despite his assurances. Meanwhile, Layla returned to the table and sat down.

"Both of you girls are young and beautiful. You're my pride and joy, full of promise, love, intelligence—lots of good things. Sure, you have some things to figure out like the rest of us do. And that's OK. Being imperfect doesn't mean that you're broken. It just means that you're still figuring things out. Understand?"

"Yes, Daddy, we understand." Layla looked at Jamie and smiled.

"And there's one other thing. Maybe I didn't tell you this enough when you were growing up, but you need to know that you are extremely valuable. You're priceless! You're like the oxygen that everyone needs to survive. And no mistakes you make now or ever at some point in the future can diminish that. It's extremely important that you know it."

"Thank you, Daddy." Jamie felt a small spark of pride in her soul for the first time that morning. In fact, it was the first spark in a few weeks.

"Now I expect you both to go out into the world and take it by storm. And by God, I know that you won't disappoint me."

# CHAPTER 12

*If a flower's perfume is the fragrance of love, does love fade with the scent in the winter?*

THE JAMIE WHO arrived at work the next day was still clinging to some of the spark that her father had ignited yesterday morning, but she was also resigned to her fate. She understood that she had a host of lumps coming her way. She might even lose her job, but Daddy was right—she wasn't perfect, much as she hated that fact. And today she would endure the consequences of her imperfection when she spoke with Tom, who was unlikely to show any mercy or forgiveness for her oversight. Jamie did not have Randall's privileges. And due to the amount of money that the company stood to lose, she foresaw a written warning, a precursor to termination and a clear signal that she needed to find another job—fast. It was a gut-wrenching reality that Jamie choked on every time she thought about it.

She had barely settled in at her desk when Hyo arrived and came into her office to check on her. He was obviously concerned about her health as well as the bits and pieces of the altercation between her and Ken that he had overheard a couple of days ago. Jamie reassured him that everything was OK but cautiously avoided going into any details about the rift, asking only that he maintain the utmost discretion with whatever impressions he had gleaned. Hopefully, Hyo's loyalty to her outweighed any impulses he might otherwise have to discuss the disagreement with anyone at the office, but Jamie was less inclined these days to count on loyalty from anyone.

After Hyo returned to his desk, she halfheartedly scrolled through her e-mail inbox and noticed that Ken had sent a few notes to her. As Tom had anticipated, Ken had hit the ground running with a few new product ideas that he wanted to build out. And now some members of Jacob's team were assisting Ken with the market analysis piece while Julia helped with comparing Ken's ideas with the performance of similar products that had been launched. With all of these ongoing activities, it wasn't unusual for Jamie to be looped in on some of the communications between Ken and Julia to ensure that Jamie was aware of any key decisions or findings that emerged. Jamie decided to read those e-mails later that afternoon—if she still had a job—since none appeared to be urgent.

She quickly scanned the remaining subject lines associated with Ken's e-mails. Her attention was unexpectedly riveted to one in particular: "Call me ASAP on Thursday." She opened the e-mail and found that she was the sole recipient, which meant that Ken wanted her to call him. Puzzled as well as edgy, she dialed his office extension, expecting that he would be unavailable, but he answered the call before the phone rang twice.

"Kenneth St. John," he announced.

"Hi, Ken. It's Jamie. You—"

"Jamie! Got a minute? I need to speak with you."

"Oh. OK, sure. I have a meeting in ten minutes, so we can speak now or wait until—"

"Ten minutes is fine. I'm coming over." He hung up before Jamie could respond. By now, her emotions were too numb for her to react with more than confusion. She didn't know what to make of his behavior.

Seconds later, Ken strode into her office with Hyo following closely behind him and immediately placing himself directly between Ken and the front of Jamie's desk as though he was guarding her from certain danger. With his back to Jamie, Hyo made eye contact with Ken, which was no easy feat since Hyo stood at five foot seven compared with Ken's muscular six feet. Hyo's atypical aggressiveness was actually a little comical to Jamie, who couldn't help smirking as Ken looked bewildered, although hardly intimidated, by Hyo's demeanor toward him.

"Jamie, I tried to tell Mr. St. John that you cannot be disturbed because you need to prepare for a meeting that starts in ten minutes, but he wouldn't let me finish my sentence."

Jamie stifled a giggle at Hyo's courage and responded to his back since Hyo had yet to break eye contact with Ken. "That's fine, Hyo. I spoke to Ken just before he came over."

"OK." Hyo continued to stare at Ken, who intermittently gave Jamie ambivalent looks. "Will there be anything else before I leave, Jamie?"

"No, I'm good. Thank you."

"OK." Hyo squinted his eyes at Ken as though expressing a warning before stepping around him to leave the office. "Do you want the door open or closed, Jamie?"

"You can close it. Thanks again, Hyo."

As Jamie and Ken both watched, Hyo walked out and very slowly closed the door behind him.

"What's with him?" Ken asked, bemused.

Jamie sank back into her chair. "He overheard our argument the other day, and I think that he wants to protect me from you."

"Why? He thinks that I'm going to hit you or something?"

"I don't know what he thinks. And I don't know exactly what he heard, so I'm not asking him."

"Well, I didn't come in here to talk about what happened a couple of days ago, but I do need to apologize for the way that I behaved. It won't happen again."

"Yeah, I guess that we both have a lot we could apologize for."

Ken paused uncomfortably. "So Hyo overheard us, huh?"

"He sits right outside of my office, and the door wasn't fully closed. He would've had to be deaf to have heard nothing, but who knows how much?"

"Jamie, I'm sorry about that. I just saw the roses on your desk and lost it. If I've caused any harm to your career here, I'll never forgive myself."

"I appreciate that." She frowned at the potential hazards that may now exist depending on whatever Hyo had heard. Normally, this concern would have been the first that leapt to her mind, but she had been more upset about the dissolution of her and Ken's relationship. It was a telling shift in her perspective that she kept to herself. "I'm hoping that he's too loyal to me to stoop to office gossip about it, but I haven't had a lot of luck in the loyalty department around here."

"Well, again, I apologize. I'd hate to do anything to besmirch your good reputation at the company. I know how you feel about all of that."

"I think that I've taken care of besmirching my reputation all by myself. In fact, I'm meeting with Tom in a few minutes to talk about it."

"You mean about the Postern forecast?"

"Yeah, I have to take responsibility for the error. I should've caught it a long time ago, and there's no excuse for how badly we overshot our projections."

"But I thought that your deadline was tomorrow."

"It is, but—"

"Do me a favor and ask Tom to extend your team's research deadline to Monday instead of tomorrow. Don't say anything else to him about it today."

"Why? The evidence is very clear that I screwed up. I may as well take the whipping now instead of putting it off."

"No, tell him that you need the extension. I spent some time with Ivan while you were out yesterday, and—by the way, are you feeling better?"

"Yes, I'm fine, thanks for asking."

"Good. Anyway, I asked Ivan to look into a few things for me, and I need a little time to chew on the information he gave me."

"Ken, I'm confused. What's going on?"

He looked past her toward her window for a split second and sighed. "I don't know, but I'm beginning to realize that something just doesn't smell right. It's really amazing what people will say in front of me because they don't know how well I know you."

"OK, and?"

"Jacob. I think that you were right about him having it in for you. He and I were talking about all of the research that your team has been doing into the Postern revenue forecast, and he mentioned that you should be fired for the mistake. And he also said something about how elementary the mistake was and that you're overpaid to do a job that a high school dropout could do better."

Jamie was floored. "Why would he say something like that? What have I ever done to him?"

"I don't know, but talking to him made me look at myself and the way I treated you the other day when you were asking for help. Friends don't do that to each other. And it's obvious that Jacob is not your friend."

Jamie hung her head, and her shoulders slouched. "I just had the guy read all wrong, which shouldn't surprise me, I guess." If Jacob was comfortable making such meanspirited comments about her to Ken, who he hardly knew, she couldn't begin to imagine what sort of degrading comments he had probably made to Tom. And now she was planning to walk into Tom's office and validate all of them.

"He just seems to have a personal vendetta against you, and I don't get it. That's why I want you to get the extension from Tom. Just one business day, OK? Let me see if anything Ivan gave me jumps out at me since I wasn't involved with any of the projections. I might find something that you and Ivan don't see because you were too close to it."

A one-day extension before she placed her head on the guillotine. She again sighed heavily. "All right. I'll ask him when I go into his office in"—she looked at the clock on her computer—"right now." She dutifully stood up and straightened her suit jacket.

"OK. I'll let you know what I figure out, which might be nothing."

"Thank you, Ken. I don't think that you'll find anything, but I appreciate the help." They both walked toward the door, and Ken opened it.

"I told you that I'm not your enemy."

"I remember. And I'm sorry that I didn't hear you." She needed to apologize for much more, but now wasn't the time.

Ken held her eyes for a long moment, but then she sensed him shutting back down before hastening back to his office as she went in the direction of Tom's. She was truly relieved and grateful that Ken had decided to help her, but there was no mistaking his continued emotional reserve. While he wanted to help her, he was careful not to insinuate any interests beyond that.

The breakdown in her relationship with Ken plagued Jamie for the remainder of the workweek. So much had happened in so short a time, and yet she remembered it all in slow motion, each catastrophe after another that had brought them to this place. People often said that hindsight was always twenty-twenty. And there was certainly a treasure trove of lessons to be found in retrospect. But Jamie's emotional turmoil was so great that she would prefer that her hindsight be entirely erased along with all memories of Ken. She would love to have a spotless mind, an ideal solution that was nowhere close to being an option. And so she tested a different option—completely blocking Ken from her mind as she got dressed to accompany Layla to Pazmeel on Saturday morning. According to Layla, she and Reed were planning to unveil a surprise that Layla had steadfastly refused to divulge. Layla was so excited about it that Jamie had not had the heart to refuse visiting the restaurant. At first, she was apprehensive about seeing Reed, who she had vigilantly avoided like a blazing wildfire, but then she realized that she was repeating her mistakes with Ken, shutting out someone who had unintentionally challenged her rigid perspectives and habits. She didn't need to be so closed-minded that she ousted people from her life for that reason, a lesson she would definitely heed from now on.

Layla had already left to drop off the kids with Mama before heading to the restaurant. The house was now perfectly quiet as Jamie began to apply mascara, her mind initially focused on the task at hand but then, despite her determined barricade, slipping away to a different time that was not so long ago in San Francisco, where she and Ken had enthusiastically explored the sights as well as each other. She had been brushing mascara onto her eyelashes in the bathroom when he had appeared behind her.

"You really don't need that makeup. You're a beautiful woman as you are."

"When I look at myself, I only see the flaws." She had smiled while continuing to apply the thick black goo.

"When I look at you, I only see the good stuff. You don't have to be perfect for me."

Jamie was jolted from the memory, her hand paralyzed midair with the mascara applicator just above her left eye. "You don't have to be perfect for me." Those words were nearly identical to her father's. Ken had wanted to be a good guy for her. But she hadn't seen it because he had shown up at the wrong time, a time when she had been intent on finding every fault about him that would hold her emotions at bay. He was too young, too egotistical, too this, too that. She was an expert at finding fault with everyone else, but the truth was that she should have been looking at herself. As Reed had said, she was her own problem. The symptom was her poor choices in men. The outcome was her perpetual doubt in every man she met. It was all self-inflicted, so if everything seemed like it had gone wrong lately, the woman in the mirror was to blame.

It occurred to Jamie that, with all of her emotional baggage, she was not worthy of Ken. Nor was she worthy of Reed's affections. And yet Reed was asking for a chance with her. He wanted to treat her the way she wanted to be treated. If she followed her mind and ignored the silence in her heart, it seemed perfectly right and rational that Reed should have his chance, especially since he had broken his bank to buy her so many roses earlier that week. And he seemed certain that his divorce was imminent. Why not go out with Reed? Why not?

Jamie looked at herself in the mirror and spoke as though to a completely different person. "Let's give Reed a chance." That unremitting silence ensued inside of her. "I'll take silence as agreement," she told her reflection. Again, no response. Jamie pretended that she was stepping into the reflection, assuming a new identity, and shedding the heartache that arose whenever Ken's reflection seemed to be superimposed over her own. This other Jamie then finished applying mascara, quickly checked the results, and left the house for Pazmeel.

When Jamie arrived at the restaurant, Reed and Layla were already waiting for her. After Reed let her in, he locked the door and broke into an ecstatic smile with Layla as Jamie's jaw literally dropped at the transformation that had taken place inside the restaurant. The dark wood-paneled walls were gone, painted over with a cream-colored shade, a simple change that had brought light and life to the entire dining area. And while the carpet was still maroon, the color actually worked now that the res-taurant windows had been decorated with sheer golden curtains that brought out the same shade of flecks that had previously gone unnoticed in the carpet. Jamie could hardly believe that she had just walked into the same res-taurant that she had visited a couple of times in as many weeks.

"So what do you think?" Reed was all teeth as he watched Jamie's reaction.

"I think that it's beautiful. It's absolutely beautiful." Jamie began to walk around the area, touching the cur-tains and more closely inspecting the walls as Reed and Layla followed.

"I told you that she'd like it!" Layla lightly elbowed Reed.

"Your sister is a mule, Jamie." Reed chuckled. "And now I know how similar you are because you're both equally stubborn."

Jamie and Layla grinned knowingly.

"I'd like for you to find one person in our family who agrees with that!" Jamie laughed while again appreciat-ing the changes to the restaurant interior. The space was much more inviting. "You didn't think that I'd like the changes?"

"I didn't know." Reed also gazed around proudly. "It's a big difference from how it looked when you first visited. Layla thought that we should consider painting the walls because it was too dark in here. I thought it looked OK, but I'm open to a different perspective since I have the leeway. I told you that the owner is relying on me to help get more customers in, and painting the walls didn't cost too much. Hopefully, it will help to lure in more people and more dollars."

"So this was your idea?" Jamie proudly patted Layla's shoulder.

"Yep. I started fussing about the decor after my first day. It was terrible!"

"Layla, you started fussing on your first day, not after it." Reed looked at Jamie, still smiling. "She didn't waste any time hounding me about the walls. I had to call the owner for his authorization to paint them just to shut her up."

"When did you get everything done?"

"We had a crew in to paint the walls on Thursday night, and then we had the new curtains installed yesterday before we opened."

"That's really amazing. And those two changes—the paint and the curtains—have completely changed the mood in here. I think that your customers are going to like it."

"That's what I told him," Layla agreed. "If you want more customers, you've gotta make the place appeal to women. If the women like it, they'll ask their men to bring them here for dinner."

"Or they will bring themselves." Jamie's independent streak flared up.

"Right, but one way or the other, women are the key, I think, to an expensive restaurant like this one being successful," Layla confidently declared as Jamie nodded.

"Makes sense."

"Well, I'm glad that you two agree with each other," Reed teased. "And if the customers agree with you, the cash register will soon be ringing more often, and I'll be hiring more people."

"Reed, is the restaurant website going to be updated with photos of the new dining room?" Layla sounded more like a restaurant manager than a sous chef, and Jamie was impressed.

"Martin already updated the website yesterday after the curtains were installed." Martin was the actual restaurant manager.

"OK, that's good. I'll check it out after my shift ends."

"You do that, colonel." Reed was clearly very comfortable with and humored by Layla's zest for the restaurant. And Jamie was getting her first glimpse at how well the two were getting along. Layla had already mentioned that Reed was treating her with a surprising amount of respect and trust, as though he had known her for as long as he had known Jamie.

Layla turned to her sister. "Jamie, I need to go into the kitchen to start prepping things for the lunch menu.

Thanks for coming out here this morning to see the changes we've made!"

"I'm glad that I came. It's awesome!"

"You really like it, huh?"

"Layla, you already know that I would tell you if I didn't."

"Now that I definitely believe," Reed joked again.

"All right." Layla smiled giddily. "I knew that you'd like it, but it's still nice to hear it." Now she turned to Reed. "Thanks for taking my suggestions. I appreciate your open mind."

"Woman, you hounded me! I had no choice!"

Layla laughed and headed toward the kitchen, leaving Jamie and Reed alone.

"You've got a great sister there, Jamie. Hard to believe that she's married to such a deadbeat."

"Tell me about it. But she's going to be all right. And this opportunity is just the beginning of her new journey, thanks to you. I've never seen her with so much confidence."

"Yeah, she's already one of the best on my staff. I'm going to make sure that she's successful here so that she can afford to make some changes in her personal life. She shouldn't be tied down to that idiot husband of hers."

"I'm glad that she's working out so well for you. She already loves the job." Jamie paused, peering up at Reed's face and trying to focus on him, his eyes, his features—but she kept seeing Ken's face, his skin, his lips. God, she missed him! But this was Reed, she reminded herself. Reed. And

Jamie deeply appreciated both his character and his innate kindness. "Reed, I—"

"Jamie"—he cut her off, apparently not realizing that she had spoken at all—"I'm glad that you came here this morning. After last weekend, I was worried that you wouldn't."

"Yes, well, last weekend was pretty surprising. You said some things that I wasn't expecting."

"And I want to apologize for that. I've tried to reach you a few times since then because I knew that I was out of line. I sincerely hope that I haven't ruined our friendship."

"No, Reed, it's OK. I've had time to think about it, and I'm OK now. A lot has changed over the past week."

"It sure has. And I have you to thank. You did me the biggest favor in the world by recommending your sister for a job here. Because of her, I've had an eye-opening experience that made me decide to make some big changes in myself and in my life."

"What do you mean?" Jamie was genuinely confused by Reed's comments.

"I mean that I realized that I have a lot in common with her husband and that I've been every bit the idiot that he is."

"I still don't understand."

"Let me break it down. I've been listening to Layla talk about her husband and thinking that he only seems to care about himself and what he wants. Everything has to be his way or no way, which is a great formula for a divorce. And then it dawned on me that Lisa has been saying the same things about me for years. My wife has worn me out with complaints that I only cared about my restaurant and myself. But when you're the one being criticized, it's impossible to see the truth in the criticisms. So I'd get all defensive and puffed up because I thought that she was the problem. If she loved me, she'd support my dreams like a good wife is supposed to do. But, Jamie, I had it all wrong. I was the nitwit. I was the one going off and doing things my way without worrying about how I might be affecting her. So I'm actually no better or different from Paul." Reed now looked in the direction of the kitchen. "I don't want my stupid mistakes to break up my family the way Paul has done. And luckily I met Layla just in time to see that."

As Reed shared his revelations, Jamie felt her new self, the one who had come here to give him a chance, disintegrating. That Jamie, the one who was trying to be more clinical, less emotional, about choosing a suitor, would not be needed today. It was clear that Reed's heart had retreated to its real home. And Jamie had no place there, which was just as well. It was as it should be.

She nodded, more to acknowledge her acceptance that, once again, things had changed very quickly. "Funny how life works, huh?" She revived her Mona Lisa smile, the best that she could do as her self-pity began to reinstate itself.

"Yeah, it is. It really is."

Reed smiled broadly as Jamie began to struggle against the black hole of depression that was sucking at her heart. Images of Ken came into clear focus where Reed's face should have been. It was so ironic that Reed's sudden enlightenment was nearly identical to her own. And she would have given almost anything for the chance with Ken that Reed now had with his wife. If only Jamie could redo the past, but this time with the benefit of the hindsight that now haunted her.

Meanwhile, Reed continued happily, "After the restaurant closed last night, I called Lisa, and we talked all night. I mean, we really talked. And I apologized for being such a nut for all these years. I don't know why she put up with me for as long as she did, but I do know that I'm not letting her go. We're going to put our marriage back together and start working on how we communicate with each other. And I'm going to do better by her."

"I'm glad for you, Reed. I really am." *And perhaps a little bit jealous*, she thought. "Are you moving back to Baton Rouge?"

"No, there's nothing for me there except Lisa, so we're talking about her coming here. We think that she could find a better-paying job in Houston."

"That's good."

"Yeah, and it's all because Layla came to work here and gave me an earful of a woman's point of view about her worthless husband. I feel terrible about the way I've treated Lisa! So I decided to do something that I've never done for any other woman."

"What's that?" Jamie's voice was abnormally faint.

"I ordered a dozen red roses for her this morning. She should be getting them this afternoon. Can you believe that? Me? Sending roses?" He chuckled. "But I get it now, the whole deal about flowers. When you told me about the roses that Ken had given you, I didn't think much of it because flowers are so simple to give to a woman. Me? I'd rather do something more personal, like cook a meal for the lady. Know what I mean? Cooking is what I do. But since Lisa isn't here, I can't cook for her. So the next best thing I could think of was flowers because I want her to know that I love her. I may not be with her in Baton Rouge, but she's still the one I want standing beside me as my wife."

Reed had no way of knowing that he had just squashed Jamie's assumption that he had sent roses to her. And suddenly her sense of aloneness was just too much. Before she knew what was happening, she broke into tears. It was pathetic.

"Aw, what's wrong, Jamie?" Seeing her tears, Reed reached for her and pulled her to him. With her cheek resting against his chest, Jamie cried even harder. "Don't cry, Jamie. I know that things with Ken haven't been good, but maybe you two can work things out like Lisa and me. It's worth a shot if you care about the guy. And I think you do care about him more than you've admitted to me—and maybe to yourself."

She labored to catch her breath as Reed tightened his hold and rested his chin on top of her head. She knew that she cared for Ken, but it was too late. And as usual, Reed had illustrated that he knew her better than she knew herself.

"It's OK, Jamie. Everything will be fine." Reed was now gently patting her back. "Everything will be just fine."

She felt so crippled inside. So lost. She saw Ken's smile, felt him touching her, imagined that Reed was Ken and held him much too tightly. Finally feeling that she was overstepping decency, Jamie released Reed and stepped back as he leaned forward slightly to look into her eyes.

"Are you OK?"

She nodded, opening her purse in a futile search for a tissue.

"Hold on. Let me find a napkin for you." Reed hurried away, found a paper towel, and brought it to Jamie, who immediately used it to rub her face and eyes.

"Thank you, Reed. You're such a good friend to me."

"I'm not just your friend. I'm your big brother. And I'm so relieved that you'll still let me be that to you."

She attempted a smile. "You're the best. Really."

"Thank you. I feel the same about you." He again studied her closely. "Are you sure that you're OK?"

She nodded, now wiping her nose. "Yes, I'm fine. I'll be fine." She again reached into her purse, this time for her car keys. "I'd better go. Mama's waiting for me to pick up the kids so that she can run some errands today."

"All right." He walked with her to the front door and unlocked it. "You drive safely. And call me if you need to talk."

"I will. Thank you, Reed." Jamie walked toward her car, pausing to look back at the restaurant door. It was already closed.

# CHAPTER 13

*Flowers rely on bees and the wind to pollinate. Love relies on the whims of man.*

FOR THE REMAINDER of the day, Jamie did her best to entertain Luke and Sadie despite her shiftless thoughts and emotions. But she was drowning in despair and depression. She had lately been forced to admit several things to herself, and today she added another admission—she was lonely. Lonely. Companionless. Single. All descriptions of herself that had not crossed her mind for years because she had intentionally been too busy to think about it. But now that she had owned up to her mistakes with Ken, her godawful desolation was all that she could think about.

The mysterious roses that someone had sent to Jamie had already been sentenced to the garbage can once she resolved their origin—sort of. The bottom line was that whoever sent them didn't matter to her. As Reed had said yesterday, it was all starting to make sense now, this thing about the flowers.

As Jamie rested on her bed and stared in the direction of her television the next morning, her mind sporadically hovered between thoughts of lost love and her impending loss of credibility at work. It would be the last blow that truly left her with nothing—except even more time to be alone.

Between her dispirited thoughts, Jamie's cell phone rang, and she despondently reached for it on her nightstand to check the caller ID. It was Ken, her saddest loss. She inhaled mournfully before answering the call.

"Hey, Ken. What's up?"

"Did I catch you at a bad time?" He was overtly cautious now that he suspected Jamie of seeing other men.

"Nope, I'm just watching TV."

"Oh, good. I just wanted to ask if you could come into the office a little early tomorrow morning. I need the original contract that your team used to create the Postern revenue projections earlier this year."

"You can pull as many copies as you want off of the system on demand. Do you know how to do that yet?" Jamie was certain that the training department had provided Ken with a manual for these types of rudimentary needs.

"Yeah, and I've already done that. But I want the original copy that Alfredo distributed before he left the company."

"Why? It's the same as the copy you can run off of the system."

"Maybe, but would you just get me the original that you have, please? Before you talk to Tom."

"OK, I'll find it and bring it to your office." Jamie was mystified by the request, but she didn't have the energy to debate about it.

"Thank you. I'll see you tomorrow morning, then."

"OK, bye." Jamie disconnected the call and wondered why Ken could possibly need something from her that was already accessible to everyone without her help. She then became slightly concerned that she might not be able to locate the contract as quickly as he apparently needed it since her meeting with Tom was scheduled for nine o'clock tomorrow morning. To be sure that he got it early enough to review before her meeting, she decided to go into the office today. She didn't have anything better to do anyway.

Jamie pulled on a pair of blue jeans and a mint-green turtleneck sweater before running a comb through her hair and leaving the house. During the drive to the office, she mentally located the most logical places where she might find the old Postern documentation. While she probably had some of the information scattered under different stacks of paper on her desk, she would forgo a search in her office since Hyo would have organized all of the most basic product information in some binders stored near Ivan's office. As Jamie rarely needed to find anything without Hyo, her challenge would be to figure out which binder was the right one. If worst came to worst, she would call Hyo for help.

Upon arriving at the Radian building, she rushed in, planning to quickly find the binder, place it on Ken's desk, and go right back home. She located the row of binders in which Hyo stored an assortment of product documentation and began to scan the labels. After skimming the paperwork stored in a couple of binders, the third one Jamie checked turned out to be the charm, so she marked the first page of the contract and walked to Ken's office to leave the binder on his desk. To her surprise, Ken was sitting in his office, engrossed in something that he was reading.

"Ken, what are you doing here?" He was wearing a dark-blue sweater that closely hugged his torso, and Jamie's impulse was to tell him how good he looked—but, of course, she didn't.

"I had a thought last night that I wanted to check out." He smiled at her as his eyes traveled appreciatively from her head to her feet before falling on the binder in her hands. "Is that the Postern documentation? You could have waited until tomorrow."

"I wasn't sure that I could find it quickly without Hyo, so I decided to come in. My meeting with Tom is at nine tomorrow morning, and you said that you needed this first thing."

"Yeah, I do. Thanks." He held out his hand as Jamie walked over and gave him the binder.

"It's opened to the first page of the original contract copy that we got from Alfredo."

"OK." He began to turn the pages in search of something specific.

"What exactly are you looking for that you couldn't find on the copies in the system?"

"I'm looking for...hold on." One of his fingers moved down the page to which he had turned and stopped. Jamie remained silent while he read the paragraph that had caught his attention. "Ha! Got it!" He reached for two other pieces of paper that he placed side by side near the binder.

"Got what?"

"Come around my desk. Let me show you."

Jamie did as instructed as Ken used a pencil to place brackets around the paragraphs of interest on all three pages.

"Jamie, your friend Jacob is one bold bastard. I can't believe that he almost got away with this."

"With what?"

"Do you see these paragraphs that I've placed in brackets?"

"Yeah."

"They all outline the kilowatt-hour rates that will be applied if customers exceed their contracted allotments, and they should all be identical since they all pertain to the Postern product. But they're not."

"Sure they are. They have to be."

"Again, they should be, but they're not. Read the parts in brackets for yourself."

Jamie again complied with Ken's instructions and read the copies, soon realizing that one of the contract copies deviated from the other two. "Why doesn't this one match the other two?"

"That's the sixty-four-thousand-dollar question. The two that match are the original copy in your binder and the copy that I found in some old files that Alfredo left in the office when he retired. The one that doesn't match is a copy that I ran off of the system, and it's the version that is actually being used to establish agreements with the customers."

"OK, you lost me. How can that be?"

"Another good question. Only this time, it's one that Jacob will need to answer since a different version of the contract would have required only his and the legal department's approval after Alfredo left. The checks and balances apparently broke down, and he took advantage of it. And"—Ken again pointed to the bracketed sections—"as you can see, the contract version that we're using raises the rates to the current retail market rates when customers exceed their contracts, whereas the other two versions would have left the rates unchanged."

"And if the rates had been left flat in accordance with the original contract structure, then my team's forecasts would have been much closer to the mark, although certainly still short in light of the climate changes lately."

"They would have been short, but you could have explained that. Radian still would have lost money because we would have needed to purchase more power at higher rates than we billed to the customers, but the losses would have been far less because we wouldn't have lost so many paying customers."

"Yes." Jamie exhaled and placed her hand on her chest, astonished at Jacob's duplicity. "I can't believe that anyone could be so underhanded. Why would Jacob do something like this?"

"I don't know why he did it, but he obviously didn't think that he'd ever get caught. He's been lobbying Tom to nail you to the wall."

"How do you know that?"

"Because he told me. I didn't want to tell you how bad it was the other day, but he's been doing his best to prime Tom to fire you."

Without thinking, Jamie placed her hand on Ken's shoulder. It was the first time that they had had any physical contact since he had brought the roses to her house a few weeks ago.

"Is that why you decided to help me?"

"It was one of the reasons. I know how hard you work, and I couldn't just stand by and watch someone take you out like that. Like I said the other day, something just didn't smell right."

Jamie dropped her eyes and her head, feeling lost again, feeling alone. "Thank you, Ken. You must know that you just saved my job for me."

"Yeah, well, I'm just glad that I could help." He placed the two contract copies they had discussed into the binder and closed it such that the edges of the paper still peeked out at the top. "Do you want me to join your meeting with Tom tomorrow? I'd like to personally explain to him that we've been using a Postern contract template that Alfredo didn't approve."

"That would be great, thank you." She self-consciously removed her hand from his shoulder and placed it in one of her front jeans pockets. "Ken…" She halted, once more overcome with an intense sadness despite the reprieve, the victory that Ken had just handed to her.

Ken looked at her and waited, speaking only after several moments had passed without Jamie continuing with what she wanted to say. "What, Jamie?"

"Ken, I'm sorry. I'm so sorry about everything, for the way that I behaved when you moved here, for pushing you away, for ruining our relationship. Everything. I'm sorry for everything. And I need you to forgive me. I really do. I—" She looked into his eyes earnestly as tears began to fall. "I need you to forgive me. Please. Please forgive me."

He grabbed her hand and held it while continuing to look into her eyes. "I already have, Jamie. You know that I can't stay mad at you. You are unlike any other woman I've ever met, and I'm glad that we're friends. We are friends, right?"

She nodded and squeezed his hand. "I'm sorry that I wasn't a better friend."

"Water under the bridge. I could have done some things differently, too."

"No, you've been perfect. You've been exactly what I needed. I just didn't know it. I didn't know that I had found you when I wasn't looking. I didn't know until it was too late."

Ken released her hand and sighed, still looking at her. "Well, maybe the guy who sent you the roses will benefit from what you've learned. And I wish you the best with him. I hope he's good to you."

"But there is no guy, Ken. I thought that you had sent the roses."

"Stop it, Jamie. We're good, so let's leave it there." He abruptly stood up and walked to his door, where a jacket was hanging on a hook. "I'm going to head out now. I'm starving." He put on his jacket while he spoke. "I'll see you tomorrow morning."

"OK." In that instant, she understood the concept of a bleeding heart and knew that no bandages would work. She didn't need to run from love. She needed to learn how to recognize love when it was standing right in front of her, before it vanished into thin air. "Ken," she almost whispered before he left the office, "thanks for everything. I mean it."

"Of course. Anytime." He walked out of the office as Jamie followed a few paces behind him, stopping at her office to watch him until he turned a corner that led to the elevators. With him gone, the building was impossibly quiet. And Jamie was impossibly broken. And alone.

The next morning, Jamie should have been dancing on top of her desk since she no longer needed to fear losing her job. She should have brought in bagels and pastries for everyone in her team to thank them for so tirelessly working to uncover the Postern revenue error. At the very least, she should have called a meeting to let everyone know that they had all been absolved of any accusation of errors because the revenue forecast had indeed been legitimate based on the contract terms that should have been implemented with the customers. But when Jamie got into the office that morning, all she could think about was how much she missed Ken. Everything that she had cause to celebrate today would not have happened without him. And just as Reed had realized that his happiness depended upon his relationship with his wife, Jamie had realized that she couldn't be happy without Ken. Had she leapt into a romantic entanglement with Reed, it would have been nothing more than a rebound, a way to escape her grief over losing Ken. And such a poorly motivated commitment would not have lasted. If anything, she would have hurt Reed because she could never have felt the depth of emotions for him that she felt for Ken. She loved him. She loved him in a way that she didn't know it was possible to love a man. And her very soul was aching now that a titanic chasm had formed between them.

As they had discussed yesterday, he joined her meeting with Tom, during which Jamie was further pained to acknowledge to herself that she and Ken made a great team. Throughout the meeting, they each seemed to know when to make the right points in response to Tom's questions as Jamie detailed all of her team's research into the Postern revenue projections and Ken explained that Jacob had pushed through a revised version of the contract after Alfredo had retired. Ken had also been sure to obtain a copy of the revised contract from the legal department so that he could show Tom that while Jacob's signature was affixed, Alfredo's approval was missing, which gave Jamie the perfect opportunity to alert Tom that her team had never received a copy of the revised contract. And without the revised contract, her team's initial forecast had remained unchanged and, thus, highly flawed. It was all so simple as presented to Tom, who maintained his placid posture and called Jacob into the office to join them after he had fully digested all of the information.

Not long ago, Jamie would have enjoyed watching Jacob squirm as he now did under Tom's methodical questioning and Ken's definitive evidence against him. But today she just felt sorry for him as he tried to explain why he had changed the contract, thinking that Alfredo's version would have cost Radian too much money on the off chance that energy prices skyrocketed as they had. He had thought that the likelihood of such an event had been minute and that the pricing change would never be noticed, but the random climate variances had triggered the revised pricing strategy along with a domino effect of losses that Jacob could never have anticipated. He pleaded for Tom to understand that he had only been trying to protect the company, at which point Tom politely asked Ken and Jamie to leave the room so that he could speak privately with Jacob. And in light of the pernicious nature of Jacob's error in judgment, Jamie was fairly comfortable in assuming that she wouldn't be seeing him again after today.

Ken accompanied Jamie in the direction of her office as they speculated about Jacob's unlikely future at Radian, but they parted ways at Jamie's doorway, and she resignedly took a seat at her desk. At some point today, she would notify her team of the good news that they needed to know, but for now, she needed more time to get past the bad news that she had a long, hard road ahead as her shattered heart labored to mend itself.

# CHAPTER 14

*Just as a flower needs sunlight to survive, love needs relentless commitment and passion.*

THEY HAD AWAKENED to the sound of rain lightly drumming against their hotel window and then checked the statuses of their flights back home. Were it not for the rain, they would already have been getting dressed for a quick breakfast before going to the airport. But since both of their flights out of San Francisco had been delayed, there was no rush. And so instead they had lazily lingered in bed, relaxing in the quiet, dozing off and on, their bodies pleasantly ensnared one by the other.

"Your skin is smooth and brown like the chocolate ice cream I had yesterday," Jamie had remarked while running her hand along Ken's firm arms. She had not intended to speak her thoughts aloud, to get too close to the precipice of saying more, feeling more. She was so dangerously close to the edge of the more.

Ken had laughed with ease and buried his face into her naked chest, so willingly provided for him to rest his head. "I've never heard that before." His warm breath had nestled her skin as he pulled her insistently closer. "Ice cream." He had chuckled before kissing her breasts.

"Yes, ice cream." Jamie had joined in his laughter while rubbing his cool, creamy back. "Makes perfect sense to me." *Ken is a marvelously delicious pleasure*, she had thought, *just like ice cream*. She had been sure not to reveal this additional impression to him.

But maybe she should have. Maybe things would have turned out much differently than they had once they were whisked back to their normal lives. Those gentle moments together may have been bread crumbs that she should have followed to that ever-elusive rainbow at the end. To love. But love for Jamie had not unfolded as it so often did in the storybooks that she had read as a young child. Instead, it had crumbled beneath her own hand, too fragile to withstand her insecurities, and slipped through her fingers like fine grains of sand. In the past, she had been able to rationalize that the men she had dated were somehow responsible for the heartless demise of their relationships, but this time she knew that the fault rested squarely at her own feet. And seeing Ken every day at the office, exchanging impersonal greetings and business-related observations, only served to intensify the guilt she felt about destroying a different, more intimate future with him. While they had certainly reestablished friendly footing, there was now a permanent pall of coolness that Jamie could not penetrate as Ken maintained the distance between them. If he were willing to hear her, she would tell him that she had changed lately. She had gained a new perspective on herself, her fallibility, and her desire for love. Being alone had once been her preference, her safety net, but now she believed it was an albatross.

In an effort to forget the heaviness inside her, Jamie tried to fall back on her old habit—using her job as the old, faithful muffler. But the strategy wasn't working as well as it had for the past few years, and she found her attention wandering that evening while reading a report that required her approval.

Christmas was a mere two days away, and the office was as quiet as it had been before Thanksgiving, since half of the employees were already enjoying their long-awaited vacations. As usual, Jamie would remain in Houston since a majority of her family also resided in the city. She was a creature of habit, but she found herself yearning to break free of old habits. She was ready to take Ken's advice and start dreaming of a future that wasn't exclusive to working. She was ready.

The formal work hours were long past, and the daylight beyond Jamie's office window was slowly creeping across the landscape to meet the awaiting darkness. But tonight, Jamie didn't notice. She no longer found any pleasure in the sunset; it only reminded her that she would soon be leaving the office to return to a lonely home. And although Layla, Luke, and Sadie were still guests, they could never provide the sort of companionship that Jamie now understood that she needed and wanted. She didn't want to be alone like Mama. And maybe she did want flowers.

Jamie reluctantly returned her attention to the report, which described a new product that Ken's team was finalizing. She was so proud of him and his work, as though she herself was producing the results that Tom had hoped for. Ken was already proving to be the linchpin necessary to helping Radian turn around its sliding revenues, and Jamie would not be surprised if he earned a promotion next year despite being so new to the company. After identifying the Postern contract pricing changes that Jacob had made, Ken had immediately worked with the legal department to restore the original contract terms as well as to implement retroactive pricing corrections for all other customers who had enrolled in the product. In an additional effort to entice customers who had altogether switched their service from Radian to competitors, the marketing team then initiated an outreach campaign that offered the customers temporary pricing terms that—based on the competitor contracts that had so far been collected in response to Jacob's idea—were better than any other products available on the market. In the short term, Radian would lose a hefty profit, but the long-term goal was to rebuild the customer base, which would ultimately rebuild the profits down the line. Everyone expected that the reparations under way would never again be needed since Jacob's firing had sent a strong message within Radian that any future disregard for corporate policies would not be tolerated.

The words on the paper before her kept turning into mere blurs, and Jamie's attention was easily drawn to the sound of something squeaking outside of her office.

She wasn't sure what it could be, but the noise was getting louder, indicating that something was getting closer. When Michael, the mailroom clerk, eventually appeared in her open doorway, she was already looking up and waiting to see what and who crossed the path. It turned out that the squeaking noise had been a loose wheel on the cart that he pushed in front of himself as he made his final round for packages that needed to be shipped that night.

"Hi, Miss Dubois," he cheerfully greeted Jamie. "Do you have any packages for me to pick up?"

"Hi, Michael. How are you?" Jamie smiled despite her low spirits.

"I'm good; thank you for asking. And you?"

"Oh, I could be better, but...you know...everything can't always go the way you'd want it to."

"I know what you mean. I was hoping that I could have gotten today off, but my manager asked me to fill in for one of my coworkers who's getting married on Christmas Day."

"Christmas Day? Why get married on the holiday?"

"She said that it made everything easier since most of the family would already be together. They have to fly in from different states around the country, and she didn't want anyone to miss the wedding if they couldn't afford more plane tickets in June next year."

"That's very smart." Jamie nodded thoughtfully.

"I guess so. I'm surprised that she's actually going through with the wedding, though. She and her fiancé had a big argument a couple of weeks ago, and we all thought that the wedding would be called off. The guy even sent a hundred roses up here to apologize to her, but she put them in the garbage. So I took 'em out and brought 'em up here. I thought that someone as nice as you might like them." He glanced around the office as Jamie gasped at the information that Michael had just shared about the roses. "Did you get them? I gave them to your assistant."

"Yes, I did. So you gave the roses to me." Roses that had actually been purchased for someone else.

"Well, yeah. I hope you don't mind."

"No, it's fine. I just couldn't figure out who had given them to me. Thank you. They were beautiful."

"I wanted you to have them because you're beautiful, Miss Dubois. I probably shouldn't say that, but you are."

"Thank you, Michael. I appreciate the compliment. Really."

"You're welcome." He shuffled his feet for brief moment. "Miss Dubois, would you ever consider letting me take you to dinner sometime? I know that I'm younger than you, and I'm not as successful yet, but I'm about to graduate with a degree in engineering next year, and I'll be making a lot more money. And maybe...well, I was wondering if you'd be willing to give me a chance? I'd treat you the way a lady like you deserves to be treated, and pretty soon I'll be able to afford whatever you want, even though you probably have your own money. I mean, what do you think?"

Jamie regarded Michael with a heavyhearted smile. "I think that it's a very sweet offer, but one that I'll have to refuse. You're a nice young man, Michael, and I'm sure that you will soon have your pick of women. If I was much younger and the circumstances very different, I'd be one of those women. But thank you. I'm extremely flattered that an upwardly mobile man such as you would be interested in me."

"I understand." Michael bashfully looked at his feet before returning his gaze to Jamie. "But, hey, I had to ask." He smiled and turned to leave her office. "Have a merry Christmas, Miss Dubois."

"You, too, Michael. Be safe." Jamie watched him leave and then continued to gaze toward her empty doorway until she no longer heard the squeaky wheel on the mailroom cart. She was sincerely flattered that Michael had worked up the courage to disclose his crush to her. He was such a shy young man that she knew that it must have been very hard for him, which was why she had let him down so easily. Had he been Randall, on the other hand, she might have run screaming from her office. The word *no* just didn't seem to register with him, and she was bone tired of finding polite words to turn him down. She was bone tired of a lot of things now.

With the mystery of the roses solved, Jamie decided to pack it in for the night and go home. She was done for the day, and trying to convince herself otherwise had been futile for the past two hours. Her heart just wasn't in it. It was entirely somewhere else, wherever Ken was. Nothing seemed right without him. And even though he didn't seem to care, he had her heart in his clutches. He walked around with it all day every day; he slept with it lying beside his bed pillows and looked at it whenever their eyes met for any reason. Jamie would eventually reclaim her emotions and her whole self, but only God knew how much time that would take.

The next day was Christmas Eve, and Layla had taken the kids to Mama's house, another custom, as the two women organized the ingredients for the Christmas Day dinner that they planned to cook for a much smaller congregation of family members than on Thanksgiving Day. Also true to form, Jamie had disingenuously offered to help with the cooking and been summarily turned down. She would thus bring some sort of dessert as she always did and as everyone already expected.

While she had the house to herself, she decided to do some cleaning up to help occupy her time and her mind. The kids were constantly leaving various types of food crumbs in some of the most obscure places, and Jamie wanted to be sure that she vacuumed everything, including the furniture upholstery, before any bugs found the trail and embedded themselves in her house.

As Bear faithfully followed behind her, Jamie ran the vacuum first around her bedroom and then on the hardwood floor in the living room. She was about to enter the kitchen when Bear started barking and ran toward the front door. Unsure of the cause for his commotion, she shut off the vacuum and stood silently for a moment, tilting her head to hear any sound that she may not have heard over the blaring vacuum noise. Before long, the doorbell rang, and she guessed that it was the second time.

"Coming!" Jamie walked toward the front door unsure of who could possibly be visiting her home unannounced on Christmas Eve. As Bear continued to bark, Jamie called out, "Who is it?" just before reaching the closed door.

"It's Ken," she thought she heard.

Her heart skipped a beat as her emotions quickened her breath. "Ken?" Immediately nervous, she unlocked the door and opened it, thinking that she may have misheard the name. But she hadn't. He was actually there on her doorstep. And he was smiling at her. "Ken, hi...What are you doing here?"

"Is it OK if I come in? It's pretty chilly out here."

"Sure." She stepped aside and opened the door wider so that he could enter her home. She also noticed that he was carrying a package that was wrapped with Christmas-themed paper. "Is that for me?"

"Yeah."

She closed the door and gingerly accepted the package from him as they walked toward the living room. "Thank you. I wasn't expecting to receive anything from you."

"I know, but it's something that I want you to have."

They entered the living room and sat down together on one of the large sofas, at which point Bear jumped onto Ken's lap, surprising both of them.

"I guess that he likes you." Jamie smiled.

"Thanks, Bear." Ken patted Bear's small head. "The feeling is mutual."

Now Jamie laughed at Ken's silliness. "Do you mind if I open this now, or do I have to wait until tomorrow?"

"No, please, open it now. I want to know if you like it."

"I'm sure that I'll like it, whatever it is, Ken."

"Yeah, right. I saw the way you reacted to the roses I brought to you. You didn't like 'em. So hopefully I did better this time."

"I'm sorry about that. It's just that every man who has ever brought me flowers has broken my heart. So I don't react to flowers the way most other women do, I suppose."

"And you thought that I was going to break your heart, too, huh?"

"Actually, I didn't realize that you were..." She stopped to take a breath, her heart pounding. "I didn't realize that you already were my heart. And that by hurting you, I was hurting myself." She looked into his eyes, willing her soul to speak to his the way that Charlotte had said a man would do when he was in love. Surely that talent wasn't limited to only men. "I'm just going to say it, Ken." She faltered and took a tense breath while holding his gaze. "I love you."

"I know." He reached for her hand and held it tightly while their eyes remained locked. "But I didn't think that I'd ever hear you say it."

Jamie was again compelled to apologize. "I'm so sorry, Ken. I was afraid, and I was being dumb. It's been such a long time since I felt this way for someone, and opening up myself was really hard."

"It's never easy for people to open themselves up if they're petrified of being hurt. It's the risk we all take."

"Are you willing to take another risk on me? I promise that I won't be so dumb again." She pressed the back of his hand to her cheek and then kissed it, closing her eyes and hanging on to that part of him. "I wouldn't be so stubborn."

Ken gently touched Jamie's face. "We're going to disappoint each other sometimes, but let's both promise to keep each other first from now on. I think that we both tend to let our ambitions get in the way of what's really important. And there's no job that matters more to me than you do. I should've talked to you before I joined Radian, but I let the opportunity and my own perspectives cloud my judgment. I'll do better in the future."

A thought occurred to Jamie, and she was momentarily worried. "So does this mean that you believe me about the roses that came to my office?"

Ken leaned down slightly and looked at her mischievously. "Yes. I believe you because I overheard your conversation with the mailroom guy, Michael, yesterday."

"Are you serious?" Jamie was immediately outdone, but too happy to be upset at his eavesdropping. "You nosy rascal!"

"I wasn't trying to be nosy! I was just walking by to wish you a merry Christmas and stopped at the door when I realized that you were already talking to someone else. You were really nice to him, by the way." Now Ken was being sarcastic, which prompted Jamie to playfully punch his arm. "Hey!"

"Don't eavesdrop on my conversations at work anymore, Ken."

"I won't!" He released her hand and gestured toward the package resting on her lap. "Now go ahead and open that."

"OK." While shaking her head with a large smile, Jamie began to slowly separate the tape on the various corners of the wrapping paper in an effort to extract the box beneath it all without ruining the paper.

"What are you doing? Just rip it off. Live a little."

"I can't. I've always removed wrapping paper like this." She continued to slowly undo the wrapping paper.

"OK, well, today is the day when you're going to start doing a lot of things differently, starting with the way that you remove wrapping paper." He reached over and tore the paper off of the box as Jamie shrieked. "There. Now open the box."

"You didn't have to do that."

"Yes, I did. Now open the box already!"

"OK, OK. Stop being so impatient."

"I've been patient with you for long enough."

Jamie opened the box, folded back some white tissue paper, and found a picture of Muhammad Ali standing over his rival, Sonny Liston, in a boxing match. She held up the photo so that she could see it more clearly and noticed that Muhammed's autograph was in the bottom-left corner.

"Ken, is that Muhammed Ali's original signature?" She was stunned at the gift and knew that it must have been expensive.

"It sure is. That's my favorite picture in my collection, and I thought that it would be something that you could appreciate like I do."

"I do, Ken. Thank you, but I can't accept this. It's too valuable and important."

"So are you." He leaned over and kissed her as she wrapped her arms around him, clinging to him, cherishing his closeness and never wanting the moment to end. It had been too long. But Ken pulled away to look into her eyes. "I wanted you to have this picture because it reminds me of you. You're a fighter, and you never seem to give up. I've been paying attention at the office, and I've never seen anyone so tenacious and determined to be the best. And I admire that in you. I already knew that you were an unusual woman, but I didn't know until I came to Radian that you have to put on boxing gloves when you go to work."

Jamie laughed and looked down at the framed picture that she was still holding.

"Jamie, I'm proud of you. And I love you."

She looked up, once again meeting his eyes as tears stung hers, this time with relief, gratitude, and joy.

"So I want you to have something that I love, something that just might make you think of me when you look at it, just like it makes me think of you."

This time, it was Jamie who leaned in to kiss Ken, softly, yet again willing her soul to bond with his. And this time, she felt that she actually succeeded as the warmth spread within her.

"Thank you, Ken. Thank you so much."

"You mean for the picture?" He grinned.

"I mean for the love." She kissed him again before carefully setting down the picture on the coffee table and then placing Bear on the floor. She then shifted her position closer to his on the sofa and used her hand to gently pull his lips to hers again, delighting in his scent and the feel of his hands on her body after so many weeks of separation. "I've really missed you."

"Not as much as I've missed you, Jamie." He ran his hand along the side of her body before resting it on her waist.

There was nothing more that needed to be said in that moment as they both burned for the physical closeness that no words, no language, could satisfy. And so they began to silently undress each other, with Jamie taking great care to memorize every muscle and crease on his body, loving everything about him. Before long, Ken returned her body to his command as only he could do, as he had done in San Francisco when they had resisted leaving their hotel room. But this time Jamie fully surrendered to him, to love, and to the future that she had been too afraid to believe could be hers. She was in love. And she knew that she was loved in return, a gift that made her bloom. She wondered if perhaps that was the real secret about flowers, that they symbolized love because they blossomed much the way she did now—like the most beautiful flower that had ever graced any man's sight.

KRYS BATTS IS a Texas native who has spent the last thirty years writing creatively. She published her first romance novel, *Walls Fall Down*, in 2003, and later a mystery/suspense novel, *What's Done in the Dark*, in 2014.

Krys currently lives in Dallas, Texas. Visit her website at www.krysbatts.com.